GREAT ILLUSTRATED CLASSICS

DRACULA

Bram Stoker

adapted by
Jack Kelly

Illustrations by Pablo Marcos

BARONET BOOKS, New York, New York

GREAT ILLUSTRATED CLASSICS

edited by
Joshua E. Hanft and Rochelle Larkin

BARONET BOOKS is a registered trademark of Playmore Inc., Publishers
and Waldman Publishing Corp., New York, New York

Printed in the United States of America

Contents

About the Author

Bram Stoker was born in Dublin, Ireland, in 1847. He had four brothers and two sisters. His father worked in a government office.

Bram was often sick as a child. While he lay in bed, his mother helped pass the time by telling him Irish legends about fairies and banshees and other strange things. He also read many books from his father's library.

When he grew up, Bram enrolled in Dublin's Trinity College. He made up for his sickly youth by becoming a champion athlete. He played soccer and broke records in track.

After he graduated, Stoker took a government job for a while. He was six feet tall and had a big red beard. He loved to see plays and later became a theater critic. He went to all the plays that were put on in Dublin.

In one of them he saw an actor named Henry Irving playing in Shakespeare's *Hamlet*. He and Irving became friends. Irving hired Bram to run a theater for him and to help manage his acting career.

Meanwhile, Stoker married and had one son, Noel. He wrote a book of weird tales for children called *Under the Sunset*.

Bram travelled all over the world with Henry Irving, including America. He met several American presidents and other famous people. He also became a lawyer. Around 1890 he wrote his first novel.

Bram had read a story about vampires and it impressed him very much. He spent a long time reading the folklore about these blood-sucking creatures. *Dracula* was published in 1897, when Bram was almost fifty. It became his most famous work.

In all, Bram Stoker wrote 18 books, four of them novels of the supernatural. He died in 1912 at the age of 64.

"Here's a Letter for You."

CHAPTER 1

Welcome to Transylvania!

What a long way this is from England, Jonathan Harker thought as he looked over the old hotel he had been given a room in. The old woman who kept the place looked nearly as ancient herself.

"Here's a letter for you, young man," she said, handing Jonathan an envelope.

He opened it quickly, knowing it could come from only one person—the very one who had brought him here on this strange journey.

Jonathan read the few lines it contained.

"My Friend—Welcome to Transylvania.

DRACULA

Tomorrow take the coach to the Borgo Pass.
My carriage will meet you and bring you to me.
Your Friend, DRACULA."

Jonathan was glad to read the message. It
meant his long journey was almost over. He
had travelled from England all the way across
Europe, over mountains, across rivers and
through deep dark forests. Transylvania was
one of the wildest parts of the continent. In fact
he couldn't find the castle of his host, Count
Dracula, on any map.

He was looking forward to meeting the
Count and asking him about some of the
strange sights he'd seen along the way. The
people here were descendants of the Huns and
the Turks. The men wore their hair long and
had thick black mustaches. The hills were
steep and wild. Jonathan made sure he noted
everything in his journal so that he would be
able to describe all the marvelous sights to his
fiancee, Mina when he returned.

Jonathan was a young lawyer. He had come
all this way to meet with Count Dracula, who

His Long Journey Was Almost Over.

had purchased a house in London, sight unseen.

When he asked the landlord of the hotel and the old woman, his wife, about the Count, they both crossed themselves and refused to say a word. Jonathan thought this odd. He found it even more disturbing when the old woman said to him, "Must you go, young gentleman? Oh, must you go?"

Jonathan asked her what she meant.

"Tonight is the feast of St. George. At midnight all evil things in the world have power. Do you realize where it is you are going?" she asked.

She fell down on her knees and begged him not to make the trip. Finally, she put a rosary and crucifix around his neck and told him to wear it. "For your mother's sake," she said.

The landlady talked to the driver of the coach. Jonathan looked for the words they used in a dictionary. It made him uneasy to realize they were talking of "devils" and "witches" and "vampires." He made a note to ask Count Dracula about all these local superstitions.

The coach carried its passengers out into the wild countryside, through dark pine woods. The road was rugged, yet the driver whipped the horses to go faster and faster. They climbed far into the mountains, the coach rocking on its leather springs like a boat at sea.

The Borgo Pass was a gap where the road went through the mountains and down the other side. It was surrounded by deep, thick woods. Jonathan got out of the coach. He felt himself trembling and tried to shake the uneasy feeling.

A carriage suddenly appeared, drawn by four black horses and driven by a tall man in a huge black hat, his face hidden in shadow. He held out a hand to help Jonathan into the carriage. His grip was like steel. All Jonathan could see of his face was two gleaming eyes and sharp white teeth.

The coach and its other passengers continued on, leaving Jonathan alone in the carriage with its strange driver. Suddenly he felt very

He Almost Jumped from the Carriage.

cold, a strange, lonely feeling.

"The night is cold," the driver said. "My master, the Count, asked me to take good care of you. Here is a rug to keep you warm. Under the seat you will find some plum brandy."

Somewhere in the distance a dog howled. Then, farther off, another answered. A minute later another, a sharper howl echoed through the mountains—a wolf. The horses reared up and plunged. Jonathan was so scared he almost jumped from the carriage.

The carriage went on into the night. It passed through a tunnel of dark trees. The wind began to moan and grow bitter cold. Snow was falling. The howling of the wolves closed in on all sides, but the driver didn't seem worried by them.

Several times the driver stopped the carriage and ran off toward mysterious blue flames that burned in the woods. Jonathan had to rub his eyes. He could see the flame shining right through the body of the driver, as if it were made of glass.

The carriage stopped again and the driver wandered far into the darkness. Jonathan waited nervously for him to return. Then the horses started to tremble and screech with fright.

"What could the matter be?" Jonathan asked himself. "I don't hear any wolves howling now."

He looked out into the darkness. When the moon came out from behind a cloud, Jonathan could see that the wolves were all around the carriage. The moonlight showed their white teeth and loose red tongues and shaggy hair. Their silence was worse than their howling. Jonathan, all alone in the dark, was so terrified that he couldn't move.

Suddenly they all began to howl, as if something had touched them and set them off. The horses jumped and reared and rolled their eyes. Jonathan beat on the side of the carriage to scare the terrible beasts away.

The wolves just came closer.

The Wolves Were All Around the Carriage.

CHAPTER 2

The Strange Castle

Just as the wolves were closing in, Jonathan heard the carriage driver approaching. The man ordered the wolves back. He shouted and waved his arm. They obeyed his command and slunk away from the carriage.

This incident was so frightening that Jonathan shook with fear as the carriage continued into the mountains. On and on they went, climbing ever upward.

Jonathan must have fallen asleep. The next thing he knew, they had stopped in a courtyard

before a massive stone building. Jonathan
again felt the driver's icy grip as the man
helped him down from the carriage. Then the
strange man led the horses through an arch-
way and was gone. Jonathan stood there alone
in the gloom.

Is this a dream? Jonathan asked himself.
What kind of strange adventure have I gotten
into? There's no knocker on this door. Will I
have to wait here till morning?

Suddenly, with a rattling of chains and a
loud grating, the nail-studded door of the castle swung back. A tall old man, dressed all in
black, stood staring at him.

"Welcome to my house," he said. "Enter
freely and of your own will."

When Jonathan stepped inside, the man
grasped his hand with a hand that was cold as
ice—the hand of a dead man. The grip was terribly strong, just like that of the carriage driver.

"Count Dracula?" Jonathan asked.

"Yes, I am Dracula. I bid you welcome,

The Count's Hands Were Most Unusual.

Mr. Harker."

The Count carried Jonathan's bags himself.

A few minutes later Jonathan sat down to a roast chicken and salad. The Count did not eat—he said he'd had his supper already—but sat and asked Jonathan many questions about his trip.

During the supper, Jonathan had a chance to study the Count's looks—the high forehead, the massive eyebrows that nearly met over his nose. His sharp teeth stuck out over his very red lips. His ears were pointed, his skin very pale.

The Count's hands were most unusual, thick and with hair growing on the palms. The fingernails were long and pointed. When one of them reached out to touch him, Jonathan felt a little sick.

Out the window, Jonathan saw the first streak of dawn. Everything was very still. But from the valley below came the sound of many wolves howling.

The Count's eyes gleamed, and he whispered

"Listen to them. They are the children of the night. What music they make!"

With that he bid Jonathan good night and left him alone to wonder about all the strange things that had happened.

When he awoke late in the day Jonathan found his breakfast waiting and a note from the Count saying he had to be out. Everything in the castle was very luxurious. The plates were pure gold, but very old. Strangely, there was not a mirror to be seen anywhere, not even in the bathroom. Nor were there any of the servants that would be expected in a big castle. Jonathan felt all alone.

He spent the time till evening in the Count's library. He found many books on England. Finally, the Count joined him.

"I have read all about your country," the Count said. "I hope you can teach me to speak your language."

"But Count, you speak English very well," Jonathan replied.

"Not so. I know that everyone in London

"The Children of the Night."

would consider me a stranger. When I move there, I want to fit in like everyone else."

"I understand," Jonathan said.

"Different countries have different customs," the Count went on. "We are in Transylvania now, not England. You may find things stange here. But tell me all about my new house."

"The estate is called Carfax," Jonathan said, showing the Count the papers for the purchase. "It has a deep, dark-looking pond, a large, very old house, and an abandoned chapel. There are only a few houses nearby. I should mention that one of them has been turned into a private lunatic asylum. But you can't see it from your house."

"I am glad the house is old," the Count said. "I could not stand a new house. I am glad, too, to hear of the chapel. That means a graveyard. I like places that are gloomy. I wish to be alone with my thoughts."

Again the Count did not join Jonathan at supper. But afterward they talked for many hours. When a rooster crowed to announce the dawn, the Count jumped to his feet.

"Your conversation about England is too interesting!" the Count said. "I forget how time flies. I must let you get to bed," he added.

Jonathan slept for a few hours. When he awoke, he began to shave, using a small mirror he'd brought with him. Suddenly he felt a hand on his shoulder. Startled, he spun around. It was Dracula.

"Good morning," the Count said.

What amazed Jonathan was that he hadn't seen the Count approach. He looked in the mirror again. It was true. The Count's image did not appear in the glass even though he stood right in front of it.

Jonathan was so startled, he cut himself a little with his razor. When the Count saw the trickle of blood that ran down his neck, his eyes blazed with fury. He grabbed for Jonathan's throat. But his hand accidentally touched the crucifix that the old woman at the hotel had hung around Jonathan's neck. He

"Away With It!"

immediately calmed down.

"Take care not to cut yourself in this country," Dracula warned. "It is dangerous. And you don't need this. Away with it!" He took Jonathan's mirror and flung it out the window. It shattered into a thousand pieces on the ground below.

Jonathan again went in to breakfast alone. He had not yet seen the Count eat or drink. A strange man, Jonathan thought, yet again.

When he finished, Jonathan explored the castle a little. He found that the building stood on the edge of a steep cliff. On three sides a stone thrown from a window would drop a thousand feet. Beyond, he could see nothing but empty woods.

But he soon discovered something else. All the doors to the outside were locked. The castle was a prison—and he was the prisoner!

When he went back to his room, Jonathan found the Count making his bed. Then he knew that what he suspected was true. There were no servants in the castle. He was alone with Dracula. In fact, Dracula must have been the driver of the carriage who had been able to control the wild wolves with his command.

He felt that he was in grave danger. He was glad that the old lady had made him wear the crucifix. It seemed to have the power to protect him.

That night, Dracula described ancient wars as if he had fought in them himself. He told stories of how his people had won great and bloody battles.

"But the warlike days are over," he said. "Blood is too precious a thing today."

Just then the dawn was breaking and the Count hurried off to bed, as he did every day.

Jonathan spent the day studying books in the library. In the evening, the Count came to him with many legal matters to discuss.

"I may want to ship some goods to a port in England," he said. "I would need a lawyer to claim them."

"We could arrange that with lawyers we know," Jonathan suggested.

"Blood Is Too Precious."

DRACULA

"Now I would like you to write to your employer," the Count said, "and to your friends to let them know you are staying with me for a month."

"So long?" Jonathan asked, his heart growing cold.

"I will take no refusal," the Count said.

Jonathan could only agree. His employer, Mr. Hawkins, had asked him to do whatever he could for the Count.

"Don't talk about anything but business in your letters," the Count warned. "Tell them you are well and looking forward to seeing them, that's all."

Dracula smiled as he handed Jonathan the writing paper. Two of the Count's sharp upper teeth hung down over his lower lip, like fangs, Jonathan thought with a shudder.

Before he left Jonathan alone, the Count said that he would be busy that night and that they would not be able to have their usual talk.

"I must warn you," he said, "that you should not sleep anywhere in the castle except in your

28

own room. You might have nightmares."

Jonathan wondered if nightmares could be any worse than being locked in this strange castle. That night he left his room and went to a staircase window where he could look out.

Just then he saw a movement. It came from the window of the Count's own room. Jonathan drew back in, then carefully looked out again.

The Count was coming out. Jonathan could not see his face, but he recognized him. And the Count's hands—certainly he could not mistake those.

Jonathan was amazed. The Count slowly came out of the window and began to crawl down, his face toward the castle wall. His black cloak spread out like wings. Jonathan couldn't believe his eyes.

It must be a trick of the moonlight, Jonathan thought. Some weird effect of shadow.

But it was true. Dracula was clinging to the cracks in the stones. He was climbing down the wall like a lizard!

One Door Was Not Fastened.

CHAPTER 3

Hall of Horrors

Jonathan knew that he must escape from this horrible place. He crept through the castle again, trying every door. All were locked. The Count must have the keys himself. Jonathan's only hope was to get into Dracula's room and steal them.

Finally he found one door that was not fastened. As Jonathan pushed on it, its rusty hinges let it swing back. It led into a dark wing of the castle. Jonathan knew he might not have this chance again. He tiptoed ahead into the darkness.

The loneliness of the place made him tremble. Still, it felt good to be away from the Count. He lay down on a couch and looked out the window at the lovely moonlit night. Feeling tired, he remembered the Count's warning not to sleep in any but his own room.

I won't obey him, he thought. Why shouldn't I sleep where I like?

He drowsed. Then, half-awake, he saw three women. They were circling him and whispering together. Two were dark, with piercing eyes like the Count's. The third had golden hair and gleaming green eyes. All had lips as red as rubies and brilliant white teeth.

The two dark women laughed and said to the fair one, "You go first. We will follow. He is young and strong, there will be blood enough for all of us."

The golden-haired woman came and bent over Jonathan. He could feel her breath on

I Won't Obey Him, He Thought.

him. It was sweet, but also bitter, like the smell of blood. Jonathan was terrified.

Suddenly the Count was in the room! His hand reached out and grabbed the neck of the fair-haired woman. His eyes were furious, his teeth bared in rage. He hurled the woman across the room and motioned the others back.

"How dare you touch him!" he cried. "This man belongs to me! You may content yourselves with this."

He tossed a bag onto the floor. It moved as if it contained something alive. One of the women rushed to open it. Jonathan thought he heard the cry of a child. The others gathered round. Then they seemed to fade into the moonlight.

The horror of it all made Jonathan faint.

He woke in his own bed and wondered if he hadn't dreamt the whole thing. But he knew he couldn't have. He knew that out there in the castle there were three women waiting to feast on his blood.

DRACULA

That night the Count told Jonathan to write three letters to his friends back home.

"The first will say your work is nearly done. The next that you are starting for home. The third that you have left the castle and are on your way."

Jonathan had no choice but to go along with the plan. The letters would be dated June 12, June 19 and June 29. Now he knew he had only a few weeks to live. He was doomed!

He had to get word out. Lately, he had seen a group of gypsies outside the castle. If he could get them to mail letters for him, he could contact his friends before it was too late.

I can write to Mina in shorthand, he thought. No one will be able to read it but her. And I will write to Mr. Hawkins, telling him to expect news from her.

He wrote the letters and threw them down to the gypsies with a gold piece. They took them and bowed, as if they understood. At last there was hope.

But the next day the Count came into

"It Is a Vile Thing and Must Be Destroyed."

Jonathan's room.

"The gypsies have given me these letters," he said. "One is from you to Mr. Hawkins. Fine. It will be sent. The other contains strange symbols. It is a vile thing and must be destroyed."

He threw the letter into the fire.

That day some deliverymen came to the castle. Jonathan ran to his window and shouted to them. They did not understand English. They looked at him as if he were a madman. One of them said something and the others laughed. Jonathan watched them unload a shipment of large wooden boxes with rope handles.

That night, Jonathan again saw Dracula crawl down the side of the castle.

Later he heard the Count return. At the same moment a wail came from the courtyard of the castle. A woman was standing there. When she saw Jonathan at the window, she cried, "Monster! Give me my child!"

She ran to the huge door and beat against it with her fists. Above him, Jonathan heard the Count's harsh whisper.

Suddenly a pack of wolves appeared in the courtyard. The woman hardly had time to cry out. The wolves went away, licking their lips.

The next day, Jonathan made his most desperate effort to escape. Taking off his boots, he climbed out onto the narrow stone ledge that ran across the castle wall. Trying not to look down, he edged his way along until he reached Count Dracula's room.

It was empty. But he could not find any keys, only a pile of gold, and money from countries all over the world. Then he found a door that led down a stone passageway. It passed like a tunnel into the ruins of a chapel. The smell was sickly and awful.

Inside the chapel were the boxes that had been delivered. Most of them held nothing but soil. But in one Jonathan found, lying on fresh dirt, the Count! He was either dead or asleep. His eyes were wide open, but he had no breath or heartbeat. In his eyes Jonathan saw a look of such evil hatred that he couldn't stand it. He hurried back to his own room.

Onto the Narrow Ledge

Before Jonathan knew it, it was nearly June 29th.

"Tomorrow, my friend, we must part," the Count said. "You will return to your beautiful England. I hope I will see you again at Castle Dracula."

"Why can't I go tonight?" Jonathan asked, testing him.

"By all means, go if you wish," the Count said.

Jonathan hurried to the front door. He was surprised to find it unlocked. He started to pull it open. At that moment, he heard the howls of the wolves. They rushed toward the door, their teeth gleaming.

Jonathan knew there was no hope in trying to outwit the Count. He had to wait till the next morning.

The next day Jonathan again dared to cross the ledge to the Count's room. He went down into the ruined chapel. There was Dracula in his box. He looked younger, his flesh swollen as if with blood.

This is the creature I'm helping to move to London, Jonathan thought, where he will find victims without number.

In horror, Jonathan lifted a shovel and swung the blade down at that horrible face. But the eyes of the Count blazed so brightly that they seemed to turn the shovel aside. It only gashed his forehead. Then the box fell shut.

Jonathan ran back to the Count's room. Downstairs he heard the doors creak open as the gypsies came to take away the boxes. He heard them hammering the lids shut, and the sound of their heavy feet.

Now I am alone in the castle with those awful women! he thought. Those devils!

He had to get out. He ran to the window. He wouldn't stay there. This time he would creep along the ledge until he found a way to escape. Or he would die trying!

Goodbye, Mina! He thought of his beloved. He stepped out onto the ledge.

She Had Just Received a Letter from Him.

CHAPTER 4

Friends with Secrets

Mina Murray had no idea that the man she loved was being held prisoner in the castle of Count Dracula. In fact, she had just received a letter from him saying that he would be leaving Transylvania soon. She was looking forward to his getting back to England. She couldn't wait to hear his stories of the strange countries he was visiting.

Meanwhile, she decided to pay a visit to her friend, Lucy Westenra. Lucy and her mother were spending the summer in Whitby, by the seashore. Mina was finished with her duties as an assistant schoolmistress.

Lucy met Mina at the railroad station. They had been close ever since they were little girls, so it was easy for Mina to guess that Lucy had some good news to tell her.

"We've always shared all our secrets," Lucy said. "Now I have something that I'm just dying to tell you."

First Mina had to get settled in the room she would be sharing with Lucy.

"I want to take you to my favorite spot," Lucy said.

They strolled onto a hill overlooking the town. They explored the ruins of an ancient church, Whitby Abbey. Below the abbey was a large graveyard.

"I come here often," Lucy said. "It has such a beautiful view of the harbor. Isn't it a lovely spot?"

Mina agreed that it was very pleasant. They sat on a seat among the gravestones.

"But Lucy," Mina said. "Don't keep me in

"I Come Here Often," Lucy Said.

suspense any longer."

"You'll never guess," Lucy whispered. "Three marriage proposals. I'm almost twenty and I've never had any proposals, and now I have three. All from the most wonderful men."

"You are lucky," Mina said. "Who are they?"

"First, there was Dr. John Seward. He runs a lunatic asylum in London, the one near Carfax estate. He's very intelligent, very kind, and most sincere. I felt so bad refusing him. He asked me if there were another. I had to say yes."

"He sounds like a fine person."

"Yes, and so was Number Two. His name is Quincey Morris. He's an American. He's always so good-humored and jolly. When I told him I couldn't marry him, he said he hoped always to be my faithful friend. Isn't that nice?"

"Very nice, but come, tell me of Number Three. He's the one who's important."

"When he proposed, it wasn't like the others. He was all confused and I was confused and in a moment his arms were around me and he was kissing me. It's Arthur Holmwood. He's so handsome and so pleasant and so everything. I love him, Mina. I said yes."

"That's wonderful," Mina said. "I can't wait to meet him."

"I wish you could. Unfortunately, Arthur's father is sick. He had to go home to be with him. I hope he'll be able to return soon."

These words gave Mina a pang. She also hoped to see her beloved soon. But it had weeks since she'd heard from Jonathan. She was beginning to worry.

The two girls settled into a pleasant routine. They often climbed to the abbey and sat for hours, reading and talking in the pleasant graveyard.

Lucy spent time making plans for her wedding, which would take place at the end of the summer. The excitement had an effect on her. She took to her old habit of walking in her sleep. Lucy's mother and Mina agreed that it would be safest to keep the door of the girls'

"What about that Ship?" Lucy Asked.

bedroom locked at night.

But almost every night Lucy got up and tried to leave. When she found the door locked, she looked for the key.

Both girls were growing nervous while they waited for the return of the men they loved. One afternoon Lucy was more excitable than ever. Mina thought it must be because of the storm that was brewing. Waves were kicking up on the water.

"All the fishing boats are racing to reach the harbor before the storm hits," Mina said.

"But what about that ship?" Lucy asked. She pointed.

Through the mist Mina could make out the shape of a large and mysterious ship. She seemed to be sailing aimlessly, as if no one were steering. Was she going to come into the harbor? Or would she try to ride out the storm at sea? If the weather got any worse, she would be in danger of crashing into the rocks.

No one had ever seen a ship move that way. Something strange was going on.

Meanwhile, Dr. John Seward, one of the men who had proposed to Lucy, was back at work again. He was studying the case of a most interesting patient. He was glad to have something to occupy his time. He had been badly disappointed when Lucy told him she loved another. But just because he was sad, he knew he couldn't neglect his duties at the insane asylum.

The patient's name was Renfield. He was 59 years old, strong in body, but gloomy. Renfield was insane in a curious way.

At times he seemed almost normal. He loved animals. His hobby was catching flies. When Dr. Seward asked him not to keep so many of them, Renfield took to raising spiders. He got rid of his flies by feeding them to the spiders.

"Why are you so interested in flies?" the doctor asked.

"Why?" Renfield said. "Because they give me life, strong life."

Dr. Seward watched while Renfield grabbed a big, horrid fly out of the air, popped it into his

Dr. Seward Was Back at Work.

mouth, and ate it.

Soon Renfield had fewer spiders. But Dr. Seward noticed that he was making pets of sparrows. The birds would feast on the spiders.

"What I would like next," Renfield said, "is a kitten. I can play with it and feed it."

The doctor told him that he couldn't allow cats in the asylum. The next day he found that all of Renfield's sparrows were gone. There were only a few feathers left and some drops of blood on his pillow.

"He's eaten the birds raw," Dr. Seward said to himself. "I will have to study Renfield's madness very deeply. This is a most interesting case."

CHAPTER 5

Storm at Sea

The sunset at Whitby lit the clouds with brilliant colors of purple, pink, violet, and all the shades of gold. But the thunderclouds that were gathering were almost completely black. It was sure to be a terrible storm.

During the evening the wind stopped. The air grew dead calm and very hot. The only boat that could be seen was the strange ship that Mina and Lucy had spotted earlier.

"Those sailors are crazy," the people said. "They'll be wrecked when the storm hits."

The Tempest Exploded from the Sky.

DRACULA

Then all of a sudden the tempest exploded from the sky. The waves crashed into the pier protecting the harbor. The wind roared like thunder. Men could hardly stand up against the fierce gale. A thick fog swept in like a ghost.

A few fishing boats found their way into the harbor. Each one was greeted by a cheer from those watching. The waves continued to toss the big sailing ship up and down. She was headed straight for the rocks.

The waves crashed and crashed again. The ship narrowly missed one rock, then another. Then, like a miracle, it slipped past the pier and was in the harbor.

A searchlight followed the strange ship across the water until she scraped to a stop on the beach. At that moment, an immense dog jumped from the deck onto the sand. He ran straight up the hill toward the graveyard.

Everyone rushed to the side of the ship. Tied to the wheel was a dead man. No one else was aboard the vessel. She had found a way into the harbor without being guided by a living soul.

"Look," someone pointed out. "He has a crucifix tied between his hands."

"He must have been dead for at least two days," another said.

The vessel was a Russian ship called the *Demeter*. Wooden boxes filled with dirt made up her odd cargo. A Whitby lawyer had been hired to take charge of them.

The big dog was never found.

"He must have run up onto the moors in terror," said one man.

The inspectors at Whitby were anxious to read the ship's log to find out what had happened. The *Demeter* had started from the Black Sea in Russia, the log said. Everything was fine as the crew sailed toward England.

About ten days out though, the captain noted a strange event. "One of the crew, Petrovsky, is missing," he wrote. "The men think there is *something* aboard the ship."

A few days later, one of the sailors came to

"He Must Have been Dead for Two Days."

the captain. "Last night during the rain storm," he said, "I saw a strange man on deck. He was tall and thin, not like any crewman. I followed him forward, but he just disappeared."

To calm the fears of his men, the captain ordered them to search the entire ship. They looked everywhere a man could possibly hide. They found no stranger on the ship.

The next week came more trouble. Another man disappeared. The crew again became very frightened. At the same time, a bad storm swept over the ship. No one could sleep. They all had to work to keep the ship afloat.

But as soon as the sea calmed, several more men vanished in the night. The crew was almost in a panic.

They were nearing England now, but there were only four men left to sail the ship. They weren't even enough to raise and lower the sails. The ship was at the mercy of the wind. The breeze blew it into a giant bank of fog. For two days they sailed through the thick mist, not knowing where they were going.

"One night," the captain wrote, "I came up on deck to take over from the man at the wheel. There was *no one there*. All the crewmen were gone now. I took the wheel myself and called for the mate."

The mate had a wild look in his eyes. "*It* is here, captain," he said. "I saw it last night. Like a man. Ghostly pale. I thrust at it with my knife, but the knife went right through it as if it were air."

The man has gone stark, raving mad, the captain wrote. As the mate went below he said, "It must be in those boxes. I'll open them one by one. I'll find it, you'll see."

The captain heard hammering from below the deck. It went on for a while. Suddenly a terrible scream filled the air. The mate ran back on deck yelling, "Save me!" Before the captain could grab hold of him, he said, "I know the secret now!" and he threw himself into the sea.

"I know the secret, too," the captain wrote in

The Funeral of a Hero

his last entry. "Last night I saw It—saw Him! I would like to follow the mate overboard, but I must stay with my ship. I will tie a crucifix to my hands. The fiend dares not touch it. Now I am growing weaker. The night is coming on. May the saints help me . . ."

That was the end of the log. No one knew what to make of this most strange incident. The captain was given the funeral of a hero. The great dog, the only survivor of that awful voyage, was never seen again. The people of the town didn't think they would ever solve this mystery of the sea.

CHAPTER 6

A Letter at Last!

The next morning Mina and Lucy went down to the harbor to see the damage the storm had done. Waves were still crashing against the shore even though the day was bright. Mina was glad that Jonathan wasn't at sea during the awful storm. But where was he? Was he safe? Why didn't he write?

They went to the funeral of the Russian ghost ship's captain. He was buried quite near the girls' favorite seat in the graveyard.

Mina was afraid the sad event would give

Mina and Lucy Went Down to the Harbor.

Lucy more bad dreams. The poor girl did seem upset.

To take Lucy's mind off all these upsetting events, Mina suggested they take a long walk.

"We can hike to Robin Hood's Bay," she said. "It will be a lovely walk and it will tire you out so that you can sleep soundly."

They walked a long way up the coast, breathing the fresh sea air. They ate a big lunch at an inn before starting back to Whitby. By the time they returned they could hardly keep their eyes open. Lucy seemed much better, with fine color in her cheeks. She went right to sleep. Mina was relieved. Everything seemed to be fine.

In the middle of the night Mina woke with a horrible sense of fear. The room was so dark she couldn't see Lucy's bed. She tiptoed across the room and felt it. Empty! Mina lit a match and looked around. Lucy was gone.

Mina didn't want to wake Lucy's mother, who had been very ill herself. She quickly looked around the room.

"She can't have gone far," she said to herself. "She's only in her nightdress. Maybe she went downstairs."

But when she looked in the sitting room Lucy was not to be found. Mina noticed the front door standing partly open. It made her shiver to think of Lucy wandering outside in only her nightdress. She grabbed a heavy shawl and ran out after her.

The clock was striking one. Not a soul was in sight. A bright full moon lit up the town. Now and then black clouds, driven by the wind, cast everything into shadow.

Far up on the hill, in the graveyard, Mina saw a white form lying across the seat where she and Lucy spent so much time. The snowy white figure stood out in the moonlight. Just as the shadow of another cloud swept over the scene, Mina saw something dark bending over the white form. Whether it was a man or beast she couldn't tell.

She ran as fast as her feet would carry her. The town lay dead around her. The distance

The Figure Raised its Head.

seemed endless. She felt she would never reach the graveyard.

But finally she grew close. Yes, it was Lucy. And, yes, a somber figure was there, bending over her.

"Lucy!" Mina cried out. "Oh, Lucy!"

The figure raised its head. Mina could see a white face and red, gleaming eyes. She ran around the church to the graveyard entrance. When she saw Lucy again, the poor girl lay on the seat alone. No one else was around.

Lucy was still asleep. She was breathing in gasps. She hugged the collar of her nightdress around her throat and shuddered as if chilled. Afraid that her friend would catch her death of cold, Mina wrapped the warm shawl around her. She fastened it with a safety pin. She might have pricked the skin of Lucy's throat for the sleeping girl put her hand there and groaned.

Mina put her shoes on Lucy's feet. She smeared her own feet with mud so that, in case they met anyone, it would look as if she were wearing shoes. As they walked back home, Lucy awoke. She begged Mina to tell no one of this incident, not even her mother.

"With her weak heart, any shock could kill her," Lucy said. Mina thought it a good idea to keep the sleepwalking secret.

When they returned, Lucy slept soundly until Mina woke her. The adventure didn't seem to have harmed her. In fact she appeared more healthy and cheerful than she had in weeks. Mina did note that the safety pin had left two red pin-pricks on Lucy's throat. She noticed, too, a drop of blood on the collar of her friend's nightdress. When she apologized for her clumsiness, Lucy laughed and said she hadn't even felt it.

Lucy continued to walk in her sleep. Mina would lock the door at night and wear the key on a string around her wrist to make sure Lucy didn't go out again. One night she awoke to find Lucy sitting up in bed and pointing toward something outside the window.

"It's only a bat, dear," she said. A great black

Two Red Pin-Pricks on Lucy's Throat

bat flitted around in circles just outside the window. It came quite close, then flew off, headed for the ruined abbey and the grave-yard.

Another time, Lucy was tired and went to bed early. Mina went for a walk in the moon-light. Returning home, she saw Lucy leaning from her window. Mina took out her handker-chief and waved. Lucy did not wave back. She was fast asleep, leaning against the edge of the window. Next to her, Mina thought she saw a large bird. When she reached the room she found Lucy back in bed, her hand clutched to her throat. She seemed pale, not her usual self.

Still no news arrived from Jonathan. And now Mina had another worry. Lucy was grow-ing weaker day by day. The roses in her cheeks were fading. She was always tired and had trouble breathing. She continued to walk in her sleep, often leaning out the window. Mina found that the wounds from the prick of the safety pin had not healed. If anything, they'd gotten larger.

About that time the fifty boxes of dirt that had arrived on the ghost ship were sent down to London, to the Carfax estate. They were placed in the ancient chapel on the estate, as their owner had instructed.

Afterward, Lucy seemed much better, almost her old self. She and Mina even returned to their favorite seat in the graveyard. They talked for the first time of the night when Lucy had come there in her sleep.

"Do you remember dreaming anything that night?" Mina asked.

"I have a vague memory of a dark man with red eyes. I heard a singing in my ears. My soul seemed to go out of my body and float in the air. Then I thought I was in an earthquake, I was shaking so. I awoke and found it was you shaking me."

Talking of it did not upset her. In fact, she laughed about it. Mina was glad to see that her friend's cheeks were rosy again. She was the old Lucy.

More good news arrived the very next day.

Mina at Once Made Plans.

DRACULA

Word from Jonathan! But not all good. The poor boy had been ill. That was why he couldn't write. Instead, Mina received a letter from a nurse in a hospital in Transylvania:

"Dear Madam, Mr. Jonathan Harker is not strong enough to write himself, but he is improving day by day. He has been suffering from a violent brain fever for six weeks. He has had a terrible shock. He talks of wolves and poison, of ghosts and demons. He is going to need a long time to get over it. We are all impressed by what a sweet and gentle person he is. We pray for him every day. Yours, Sister Agatha."

Mina at once made plans to go to Transylvania herself. She would nurse Jonathan to health and bring him home. They would be married right away. She made her plans as quickly as she could and set off on the long journey.

About the time that the boxes of dirt were delivered to the Carfax estate, Dr. Seward, whose insane asylum was next door, noticed a change in his patient Renfield.

"The man gets excited and sniffs around the way a dog does," the doctor wrote in his journal. "He seems nervous and keeps saying, 'The Master is at hand.' He has even lost interest in his spiders and flies. This is a very strange development. I must keep a close eye on him."

That night, at two o'clock in the morning, the night watchman woke Dr. Seward.

"It's Renfield," the watchman said. "He's escaped!"

"Renfield's Escaped!"

CHAPTER 7

The Mysterious Illness

Dr. Seward alerted the guards and ran out himself to follow Renfield. He was afraid what would happen if that madman found a way out of the asylum grounds.

"There he is!" he shouted to the guards. He caught a glimpse of Renfield climbing the high wall around the asylum. He was headed toward the Carfax estate next door.

Dr. Seward found a ladder and went over the wall himself. He saw Renfield ducking around the corner of the house. He followed. In a minute he found the lunatic pressed against the door of the old chapel. He was talking to himself.

Dr. Seward approached carefully so as not to scare the patient away. As he slowly crept closer, he could hear Renfield saying, "I am here to do your bidding, Master. I am your slave."

When the guards came, Renfield fought like a wild beast. The guards had to put him into a straitjacket. They led him back to the asylum and chained him to the wall in the padded room. There he sat murmuring, "I shall be patient, Master."

Dr. Seward was relieved that such a violent madman had not gotten out where he could harm people.

Meanwhile, Mina had travelled as quickly as she could to Transylvania, first by boat, then by train. She found her Jonathan thin and pale and weak-looking. He did not remember anything that had happened for a long time. Mina

"I Feel My Head Spin Around."

knew he must have had a terrible shock. The nurses said he had spoken of dreadful things, but they wouldn't tell Mina what they were.

"Mina, my dear," Jonathan said. "When I try to think of what has happened, I feel my head spin around. I don't know if it was all real, or the dreaming of a madman. I hope that you will still agree to be my wife."

"Of course, my love," she answered. "I have sent for the chaplain. We can be married this very day."

As soon as the wedding was over, Mina sat down and wrote a letter to her friend back in England.

"Dearest Lucy, I am now Mrs. Harker. I am so happy. Jonathan still hasn't said anything about his awful experiences. He gets mixed up about what day it is, or even what year. But he is getting better little by little. I hope that you may be as happy when you marry Arthur as I am now. I must go and tend to my husband. Your ever loving, Mina."

Lucy was glad to receive this news. By the

end of her stay in Whitby, she was feeling much better. She no longer walked in her sleep. Arthur came to visit her. In another month they would be married, too.

But when she returned home to London, Lucy's bad dreams began again. Each night she tried to keep herself from going to sleep so that she would have no more nightmares. She felt worn out all the time. One night she woke to hear a scratching or flapping sound at the window. She grew horribly weak and ghastly pale. She could not get enough air. The marks on her throat were sore.

When Arthur next saw his fiancee, he was shocked. "I insist that you see a doctor," he said. "I am going to call our friend, John Seward. He'll be over tomorrow."

Before Dr. Seward arrived, Arthur had to go home to see his father, who again was ill. Dr. Seward examined Lucy and found that she had changed terribly. She seemed to lack blood. She told him she was always tired and had bad dreams every night.

She Seemed to Lack Blood.

But Dr. Seward could not find any cause for her illness. The sickness was very mysterious. Dr. Seward, who loved Lucy almost as much as Arthur did, was very worried.

"I've decided to contact my old teacher, Professor Van Helsing, in Holland," he wrote in a letter to Arthur. "Van Helsing is one of the most advanced scientists of the day. He is also very kind and generous. He might be able to figure out Lucy's strange condition."

At the lunatic asylum, Dr. Seward continued to puzzle over the case of the patient Renfield. Sometimes the man would be very violent, at other times quiet and peaceful. He was agitated during the day, but calm at night.

They took the staitjacket off him because he seemed better. But then he escaped again. This time Dr. Seward knew where to look for him— at the Carfax estate next door. When the guards came to take him back, he fought terribly. Then he suddenly calmed down. Dr. Seward saw him looking into the sky at a big black bat hovering nearby.

"I shall go quietly," Renfield said.

Professor Van Helsing arrived the next day and went with Dr. Seward to examine the patient. When he saw her, he lowered his bushy eyebrows. But he didn't tell Lucy of his concern. He talked with her about everything except her illness.

As he examined her, he said little. Dr. Seward knew it meant that he was thinking very deeply. Van Helsing was not just a medical man. He had studied philosophy and also knew a great deal about the supernatural.

Later Van Helsing said to Dr. Seward, "In all my years, this is one of the strangest cases I have seen. So much blood lost. But how? This disease interests me very much."

Van Helsing had to go back to Holland, but he promised to return in a few days. He needed to find out more about what might be troubling Lucy by checking in his library.

"Keep a close watch on the patient," he told Dr. Seward. "If her condition changes, let me

"She Will Die."

"know at once."

"But you agree that it's very serious?" Dr. Seward said.

"Oh, very," Van Helsing answered. "This could be a matter of life and death."

They could not tell Lucy's mother how worried they were about her daughter's health. Even a little shock be too much for the old lady's heart. They just had to wait and see what happened.

Lucy did not get any better. When Van Helsing returned, he and Dr. Seward both went up to her room. They were shocked by what they saw.

Lucy was pale as a ghost. The red seemed to have gone even from her lips and gums. The bones of her face stood out. Her breathing was painful. She lay motionless and did not seem to have the strength to speak.

"My God, this is awful," Van Helsing said. "She will die from lack of blood if we don't do something quickly."

CHAPTER 8

A Life to Save!

"There is no time to lose!" Van Helsing said. "There must be a transfusion of blood right away. Will it be you or me?"

"I am younger and stronger, Professor," Dr. Seward said. "It must be me."

"Then get ready at once. I will bring up my bag. I am prepared."

Before they could begin, there was a pounding at the front door. It was Arthur.

"I came as soon as I could," he said. "I am so thankful to you, Professor Van Helsing. How is

"It Must Be Me."

my dear Lucy?"

"You have come just in time," Van Helsing told him. "She is bad, very, very bad. But you can help her. You can do more than anyone to save her life."

"What can I do?" Arthur cried. "I would give the last drop of my blood to save her."

"We don't ask for that much," Van Helsing said. "But the young lady is very ill. She needs blood or she will die. We want to perform a transfusion, and transfer some of your blood into her empty veins."

"If you only knew how glad I am to do it," Arthur answered.

"Good," the professor said. "We must hurry. There is not much time."

Lucy was not asleep, but she was too weak to talk. Her eyes spoke to her beloved, but that was all.

The two doctors connected a tube from Arthur's vein to Lucy's. As the blood began to flow between them, the doctors saw a gradual improvement in the sick girl. Arthur grew pale and weak, and Lucy showed some color. But she was only partly restored. The terrible strain had weakened her badly.

When they were finished, Van Helsing told Arthur to go home and rest. "Sleep much, eat much, you will quickly regain your strength. The operation was successful and you have saved her life. When she is well, she will love you for what you have done."

After he had seen Arthur to the door, Dr. Seward found Van Helsing examining the two marks on Lucy's throat.

"What do you make of those?" Van Helsing asked.

"Two small holes," Dr. Seward said, looking closer. "No sign of disease, but not healing properly either. They look worn. Perhaps this is how she has lost blood. But if so, the bed would have been drenched with red."

"This may be very serious," Van Helsing said. "I will have to go back to Holland once again and consult my books. You must stay here with her. You must not sleep all night. Not

"Stay with Her at All Times."

a wink. Don't let her leave your sight."

"Why, what do you think it might be?" Dr. Seward said.

"I cannot say yet. Only, heed my warning: stay with her at all times. If you leave her, the result may be very serious."

Dr. Seward sat up all night in Lucy's room. In the morning she awoke and seemed much better. When he told her mother he needed to stay with her the next night, too, she said it wasn't necessary.

"She's really much improved, Doctor," Mrs. Westenra said. "And you are so tired."

"We have to trust Professor Van Helsing," Dr. Seward told her. "I dare not leave your daughter alone until he returns."

That night Lucy was tired from her illness, but Dr. Seward could see she was trying to avoid closing her eyes.

"Don't you want to sleep?" he asked her.

"I dread the nightmares that come to me."

"I will be here all night," he promised. "If I see any signs of bad dreams, I will wake you at once. You can sleep in peace."

Lucy was very grateful. She slept calmly all night and again seemed better in the morning.

Dr. Seward had to attend to his business at the insane asylum during the day. By the time the sun went down, he was as tired as a dog.

"You need not sit up with me again," Lucy insisted. "I am so much better. You lie down in the next room. If I want anything, I will call out and you can come in at once."

Dr. Seward agreed. He stretched out on the sofa in the next room and soon he was fast asleep. In the morning, Professor Van Helsing arrived back from Holland. He woke Dr. Seward and asked, "How is our patient?"

"Much better," Dr. Seward said. "She's making steady improvement."

"Let's go see."

When they entered Lucy's room, Van Helsing turned pale himself and said, "Oh, my God!"

Lucy lay in her bed, barely breathing, whiter and weaker than ever. Her gums seemed to

Soon He Was Fast Asleep.

have shrunk back from her teeth.

"All our work is undone!" Van Helsing said. "Quick, before it is too late. She needs another transfusion."

This time he drained blood from Dr. Seward into Lucy's veins. The doctor was glad to do what he could. He loved Lucy, too. But the transfusion left him weak and dizzy.

"But Professor, how could she have lost so much blood? There is no sign of bleeding. Only those two pin pricks on her throat."

Later Lucy awoke, with her health only barely restored. Van Helsing told Dr. Seward that he himself would stay with Lucy tonight.

"What is causing this illness?" Dr. Seward asked. "I have never seen anything like it."

"It may be, my friend, that it is something beyond your knowledge. Far beyond."

Van Helsing sat at Lucy's bedside all night. He studied her face very seriously. The next day, a shipment of white flowers arrived.

"These are for you, my dear," Van Helsing told her.

"Why, Professor, how kind of you."

"They are not just a pretty gift," he said. "Smell them."

She sniffed them and laughed. "Why, they are only common garlic. Are you playing a joke on me?"

Van Helsing's jaw became firm and his eyebrows joined together in an angry frown. "I never joke!" he cried. "These flowers have a most grim purpose. I warn you, do not disobey me!"

Lucy was quite startled. Van Helsing became more gentle and assured her that the garlic was for her own good, a kind of medicine.

Then he went around the room, putting garlic everywhere. He fastened the windows tightly closed and wiped garlic all around them. He hung some over the door and at each side of the fireplace. He even made a ring of garlic and hung it around Lucy's neck.

"Professor," Dr. Seward said. "It almost seems like you're working a spell to keep off evil spirits."

The Garlic Gave Her a Sense of Peace.

"Perhaps I am," Van Helsing answered. To Lucy he said, "Take care that you do not remove this necklace. Don't open any of your windows tonight. Will you promise that?"

"I promise," Lucy said. "Thank you both for being so kind."

When they were leaving, the professor said to Dr. Seward, "Tonight we can both sleep in peace. She will be safe."

Lucy drifted off to sleep. Something about the garlic gave her a sense of peace. For once she felt protected against the awful dreams that had come to her.

In the morning, Dr. Seward and Professor Van Helsing returned to Lucy's house early. There they found her mother, who usually got up at dawn.

"Lucy is so much better," she said. "She's still sleeping. I looked in, but I didn't want to wake her. She needs all the rest she can get. I am so grateful to both of you."

"Wonderful," Van Helsing said, rubbing his palms together. To Dr. Seward he said, "My precautions have worked. I think we may be getting to the bottom of poor Lucy's illness."

"I have to take some of the credit myself," Lucy's mother said.

"How do you mean, madam?" the professor asked.

"Last night I was worried about Lucy so I went in to check on her. I found that she was sleeping very soundly. She didn't even awake when I went in to see her. But the room was terribly stuffy. There were those awful, strong-smelling flowers all over the place. Even around her neck. I thought that in her weakened state the smell would be too much for her. I took them away and opened the window to let a little fresh air in. I am sure you will be pleased to see how it's helped her."

The old lady went off to have her breakfast. Dr. Seward looked to see that the professor's face had turned ashen gray.

"Oh, no!" was all Van Helsing could say.

"I Have to Take Some of the Credit."

CHAPTER 9

The Howl of the Wolf

"What have we done?" Professor Van Helsing cried. "What has the mother of this poor girl done? We cannot even let her know that she may have put her daughter's body and soul in the gravest danger."

"What do you mean?" Dr. Seward replied. "What danger?"

"No time to explain," Van Helsing said. "Come, we must hurry. We must fight these devils if we can."

He grabbed his medical bag. He and Dr.

Seward rushed upstairs to where Lucy was sleeping. When they entered, Van Helsing was not surprised by her horrible appearance. Her skin was pale and waxy. She looked worse than ever.

"No time to lose," Van Helsing said. "Another transfusion is needed. You are too weak. I must give her my own blood, old as I am."

Dr. Seward performed the operation. Van Helsing's blood brought some color back to Lucy's cheeks once again. Her breathing became more regular.

Van Helsing explained to Lucy's mother that she must never remove anything from her daughter's room without asking him.

"The scent of the garlic flowers is part of the treatment," he said. "It will make the girl better."

The next few nights, Van Helsing himself stayed with Lucy.

His presence let her sleep in peace. She began to feel as if she had been through a long nightmare and had finally awakened. She

"The Wolves Seem to Be Upset."

could dimly remember the terrible fear she had suffered, but it seemed distant now. She even grew to like the smell of garlic.

One night she awoke to find Professor Van Helsing asleep. She still felt safe, even though something again made an angry flapping sound against her window pane.

Other strange things were happening in the city at the same time. At the London Zoo, the keeper was alerted one day to a terrible howling from the wolf's cage. He ran to see what was the matter and found a tall thin man standing watching the animal. He was a nasty-looking man with a cold expression and red eyes.

"The wolves seem to be upset," the man said.

"Maybe it's you," the keeper said. He instantly disliked the man.

"Oh, no, I would never upset them," the man said. His smile was full of sharp, white teeth.

As he spoke he moved closer to the wolf's cage and thrust his hand right inside. The wolf lay down. The man scratched him behind his ears. "I am used to wolves," he said.

"Are you in the zoo business yourself?" the keeper asked.

"No," the man answered, "but I have made pets of several wolves." And with that, he tipped his hat and left.

That night, the biggest wolf in the zoo escaped! The keeper found the bars of the cage twisted and the wolf gone. No one saw any one in the zoo that night, but one guard said he thought he had seen a big gray dog.

Word went out all over London that a wolf was on the loose. All the children in the city were afraid to go outside. The next day, though, the wolf turned up back at the zoo. No one knew where he had gone. The keeper did find that the animal had been cut by broken glass.

The same night that the wolf escaped, Lucy went to bed as usual, with all the garlic flowers around her. In the middle of the night she

The Keeper Found the Bars Twisted.

woke up and heard the familiar scratching and flapping at her window. She had been hearing it since her sleepwalking in Whitby.

She was afraid to go back to sleep, afraid of the nightmares that seemed close by. She tried to stay awake, but she felt terribly drowsy. She was afraid to be alone. She went to the door of her room and called out, "Is anybody there?" No one answered.

From outside in the shrubs came a howling. It sounded like a dog, only deeper and fiercer. Lucy went to the window and looked out. She could see nothing, only a big bat which swooped up against the glass.

She got back in bed. A minute later the door creaked open. It was her mother.

"I was worried about you, darling," her mother said. "I came to see if you were all right."

Lucy was afraid her mother would catch cold, so she asked her to get under the covers with her. They tried to comfort each other.

The flapping came at the window again.

Lucy's mother cried, "What is that?"

Both of them heard the low howl in the shrubs again.

Suddenly, the window glass shattered! The curtains blew back in the wind, and a large gray wolf burst into the room.

Lucy's mother screamed in fright. She grabbed at anything she could. Her hand caught the necklace of garlic flowers that Van Helsing insisted on Lucy wearing and tore it off. She sat up and pointed at the ferocious wolf. A strange gurgling sound came from her throat. Then she fell over as if struck by lightning.

Her head knocked into Lucy's and left her daughter dizzy for a moment. The room seemed to spin around. Little flecks of light came in through the window. Lucy could not make herself move. Her mother's body lay on top of her. The old lady was dead. Lucy remembered nothing more for a while.

When she awoke, Lucy could hear dogs howling all over the neighborhood. A bell was

Both Fast Asleep

tolling. From outside came the beautiful song of a bird. Lucy imagined that it was the voice of her dead mother.

The family's two maids came running into the room. They lifted the body of Lucy's mother and laid it out with a sheet over it. They placed the flowers of garlic on the body. Lucy remembered what Van Helsing had said, but she couldn't bring herself to remove the flowers from her poor mother. Anyway, the servants could sit with her now.

But the two servants never returned. Lucy went to look for them and found that they had drunk some sherry that had put them both fast asleep.

Now Lucy was left alone with her dead mother. She couldn't close the window—the glass was broken. Outside she heard the low howl of the wolf. She became very afraid. What could she do? She would have to wait for whatever horrors were in store for her.

CHAPTER 10

Death's Kiss

The next morning Dr. Seward hurried to Lucy's house. He knocked on the door, but no one answered. He was afraid something terrible had happened. He went all the way around the house, looking for a way to get in.

Soon Professor Van Helsing also arrived. Dr. Seward explained the situation.

"I fear we are too late," the professor said. "Hurry! If we cannot find a way in, we must break in."

At the back of the house the two doctors

"We Must Break In."

were able to force open a kitchen window and climb into the house. The found the two servants still sleeping from the wine they had taken. The doctors ran up the stairs to Lucy's room.

What a sight they saw! Both Lucy and her mother lay on the bed. On the mother's face was an expression of deep horror.

Lucy was as white as a ghost. The two wounds on her throat had been opened again and looked raw. The professor ran over to listen for her heart beat.

"It's not too late!" he cried. "She's still alive."

"She needs another transfusion of blood," Dr. Seward said.

"First we must warm her," Van Helsing told him. "She is almost as cold as her dead mother. Prepare a hot bath at once."

Dr. Seward woke the maids and they heated water for a bath. They carried Lucy to the warm water and soaked her in it.

"I know this is a struggle against death," Dr. Seward said.

"If that were all it was, I would stop right now and let her die in peace," Van Helsing answered. "There is no life left for her. This is something even more serious."

Lucy's heart began to beat a little more strongly as they dried her off with hot sheets.

Just at that moment, there was a knock at the door. The visitor was Quincey Morris, Arthur's American friend. He was coming with a message from Arthur, who had had to rush to the bedside of his dying father.

"You are just in time," Dr. Seward said. In a flash, Quincey agreed to give some of his blood to Lucy.

"I am glad to help her," he said. "I also loved that little lady and wanted to marry her."

The two doctors prepared for the transfusion. Lucy improved, but only slightly.

"How is this possible?" Quincey asked when the operation was over. "How could she receive the blood of four strong men in a matter of days? Where did it all go?"

"I can't even begin to guess," Dr. Seward

Quincey Morris Patrolled Outside.

said. "This is one of the deepest mysteries I have ever come across."

That afternoon Lucy finally awoke. She seemed a little better as she looked around the room. But all of a sudden she gave a loud cry and began to weep. She remembered now that her dear mother was dead.

The whole of the afternoon she spent in low spirits, sobbing now and then in her grief. About sunset she eased into a light sleep. She slept fitfully all night as the two doctors took turns watching her. Quincey Morris patrolled around the outside of the house in case the wolf returned.

In the morning she seemed weaker. She could hardly turn her head and would eat almost nothing. She frequently drifted off to sleep. Dr. Seward noticed how haggard she looked. Her teeth appeared longer and sharper than usual.

They sent a telegram to Arthur. He rushed back to London. He was shocked when he saw Lucy's face. He wanted to stay with her every minute, but Professor Van Helsing insisted that he get some rest.

They had moved Lucy into another room where they could lock the window. Again, the professor put flowers of garlic everywhere.

As Dr. Seward sat with the poor, sick girl, he noticed that her teeth were even sharper than in the morning. The two canine teeth were longer than the rest and sharply pointed.

What is that flapping sound at the window? the doctor asked himself. He went to see. It was a big bat that kept scraping against the glass. When he returned to Lucy he found that in her sleep she had torn the garlic from around her throat, as if she couldn't stand it. He replaced it as best he could.

At dawn, Van Helsing came to relieve Dr. Seward. He took a careful look at Lucy and suddenly drew in his breath.

"Hurry, open the curtain," he said. "I need light."

Dr. Seward drew back the curtain. He rushed back to the bedside. Van Helsing was

It Was a Big Bat.

examining Lucy's throat. "Look!" he said. The two wounds had absolutely disappeared.

"What does it mean, Professor?" Dr. Seward asked.

"She is dying! All that matters now is whether she dies awake or asleep. Tell Arthur to come right away."

Dr. Seward hurried to where Arthur was still asleep.

"Call on all your strength now, my friend," he said. "I'm afraid that the end is near."

When they reached Lucy's room they found that Van Helsing had brushed her hair and made her look a little like her old self.

"Arthur my love," she whispered. "Come near."

Arthur, with tears in his eyes, sat near Lucy's bed. He held her hand as she drifted off to sleep. Her breathing became heavy and Dr. Seward again noted her long, pointed teeth.

When she awoke once more, she said, "Kiss me, Arthur. Please kiss me."

"No!" Van Helsing said. He grabbed Arthur

by the neck and pulled him away. "You must not kiss her!"

Arthur was startled. What could this mean?

"Thank you," Lucy whispered to the professor. "You are a true friend. Guard him from me. And give me peace."

"I will, I swear," Van Helsing told her. To Arthur he said, "Kiss her once, but only on the forehead."

He did so. Lucy's breath grew harsh again. Then it stopped.

"She is dead," Van Helsing said.

Dr. Seward led Arthur into another room. When he returned he found Van Helsing studying Lucy's face. Death had restored much of her beauty. She seemed less pale than she had during the difficult weeks of her illness.

"Well, poor girl," Dr. Seward said, "at last you are in peace."

Van Helsing turned to him and with a grave and solemn voice said, "It is not so. This is only the beginning!"

Searching for Some Clue

CHAPTER 11

Dracula in London!

They arranged Lucy's funeral for the next day so that she and her mother could be buried together.

Dr. Seward and Professor Van Helsing went through all of Lucy's papers and read her diary, searching for some clue about the terrible things that had happened.

"We should go and get some rest," Van Helsing said as night fell. "We still have much work ahead of us."

Before going to bed, they went in one more

time to look at the poor girl who had died. A sheet had been pulled over Lucy's face. When Van Helsing lifted it, both he and Dr. Seward drew back in surprise. All of the loveliness that Lucy had had in life had come back to her. There was not a trace of illness.

"I cannot believe my eyes," Dr. Seward said.

But the professor only looked grave and worried. "Stay here until I return," he said.

He went out and came back with more garlic flowers. He placed them with the other flowers that had been put near the body. He took a small gold crucifix and placed it over her mouth. Then he pulled the sheet back to cover her face.

"Professor," Dr. Seward said. "I've always thought of you as a sane and reasonable man. But I can't understand all these mysterious things that you do."

"Do I ever do anything without a reason?" Van Helsing asked. "You were surprised that I would not let Arthur kiss his beloved. But she thanked me for it. You must trust me, John.

Both Drew Back in Surprise.

There are strange and terrible days before us.
We have to be united."

Dr. Seward took Van Helsing's hand and
promised to help him any way he could.

The next day before the funeral Arthur came
to look once more at the woman he loved.

"How beautiful she is!" he said to Dr.
Seward. "I am amazed. Is she really dead?"

Dr. Seward assured him she was. But even
he was astounded by Lucy's appearance. She
seemed to grow more and more lovely every
hour.

Arthur kissed Lucy's hand and kissed her on
the forehead. Then they put the lid on the coffin and screwed it in place.

In Exeter, many miles to the west of London,
Mina and Jonathan Harker had also been to a
funeral. Mr. Hawkins, the lawyer that
Jonathan worked for, had died. Now the firm
belonged to Jonathan. It kept him very busy.

He had to go to London to handle some legal
affairs. He took Mina with him. One evening

they were walking along the street looking in
the windows of all the shops. Suddenly
Jonathan gripped Mina's arm so hard it hurt
her.

"What is it?" she asked.

"My God!" Jonathan said.

Mina saw that Jonathan's eyes were bulging
from his head. He was staring at a tall, thin
man.

"Do you see who it is?" Jonathan whispered.

"No, dear, I don't know him," Mina said.
"Who is it?"

"It is the man himself! It is the Count! But
somehow he has grown young! Can it be?"

The man moved on. Jonathan remained very
upset. Mina was afraid his brain fever would
come back. But the next morning, he seemed to
have forgotten all about the incident.

Mina was troubled. She wasn't sure if the
things that Jonathan had recorded in his Transylvania diary had actually happened, or
whether they were just in his imagination. She
remembered that he had gone out there to help

She Buried Her Face in Her Hands.

the Count move to London. What if everything he said was true? What if Dracula was now in London, where he could prey on millions of people?

When they returned home to Exeter, Mina found a telegram waiting for her. As soon as she read it, she buried her face in her hands and cried.

"What's the matter, darling?" Jonathan asked.

"It's Lucy," Mina cried. "She's dead. And her mother, too. They are to be buried together today."

"How awful," Jonathan said. "That poor girl. Who is the telegram from?"

"It's from a man named Van Helsing," she said, "whoever that is. He would like to come and talk to me about Lucy. He says it's very important."

The next day Van Helsing arrived in Exeter. Mina was anxious to meet him. She hoped that a man of such learning could also help explain Jonathan's strange experience.

"I have read your letters to Miss Lucy," Van Helsing told her when he arrived. "You mention a time when you saved her from sleepwalking in the graveyard. That interests me very much. I wish you would tell me everything about it."

Mina was glad to give the professor all the details. It was the first time she had told anybody about Lucy's odd adventure.

"Your account clarifies many things," Van Helsing told her when she had finished. "What you have said may be very helpful. If there is anything I can do for you, please ask."

"There is something, Professor," Mina said. "My husband has suffered from brain fever, which came over him when he was in Transylvania. It still bothers him very much. If there is anything you can do to put his mind at ease, I would be very grateful."

"Tell me all about it," the professor said.

"You must first promise not to laugh at me," she said. "These events were so strange they hardly seem possible."

"He Was in Transylvania."

"Don't worry," Van Helsing assured her. "If you only knew the strange things that I have gone through with your friend Lucy, you would be sure that I have an open mind."

Mina related all she knew about Jonathan's trip to Castle Dracula. The old professor was fascinated by the details and asked her many questions.

"One thing I can promise you," he said when she had finished. "All that happened to your husband is true! He need not have doubts about it. I must talk with him as soon as possible."

"He's away on business," Mina said. "But I'm sure he'll be happy to see you. Only one thing, Professor."

"What is it?"

"If everything that happened to Jonathan is true, it means that Count Dracula is in London now. That monster is free to prey on all those innocent persons."

"Very true," Van Helsing said. "And we must take action right away. You and your husband could be a great help."

"We'll do all we can," Mina promised.

Back in London, Van Helsing met with Dr. Seward.

"I have just read a story in the paper that disturbs me very much," Van Helsing said. He handed it to his friend to read.

It told of several young children who had been missing recently in London. When their parents found them, the children each told of a "beautiful lady" in white. They seemed all right, but were somewhat weak and pale.

"We must go see these children at once," Van Helsing said. He and Dr. Seward went to the hospital where one of the little victims was being treated. They knew the doctor there, and he let them examine the child.

"What do you see?" Van Helsing asked.

"Puncture wounds," Dr. Seward said. "They look very much like those on Lucy's throat. Do you think they could have the same cause?"

"Not the same, no," Van Helsing said. "Let

"Miss Lucy Herself!"

me ask you, John, do you think it's possible that things can happen that science cannot explain?"

"I am a man of science," Dr. Seward said. "I think everything has an explanation."

"But what about hypnotism?" Van Helsing said. "Didn't that seem strange at first? What about those bats in South America that can drain the blood of a horse?"

"Do you think Lucy and these children have been bitten by a bat?" Dr. Seward asked.

"No," Van Helsing replied. "I only want to prepare you to believe what you cannot believe. You said that maybe the marks on the children came the same way as Miss Lucy's wounds. I tell you, it is not so. It is worse. Much, much worse."

"What do you mean, Professor?"

"Those marks were made by Miss Lucy herself!"

CHAPTER 12

The Un-Dead

"Dr. Van Helsing, are you mad?" Dr. Seward cried.

"I wish I were," Van Helsing said. "I assure you, I would do nothing to offend the memory of Miss Lucy. But if you come with me tonight, I will show you something that will prove what I say."

Dr. Seward did not want the professor to prove such an awful thing about a woman he had loved, but he agreed to go. The two men had dinner together, and then set out for the

The Two Men Set Out.

graveyard where Lucy was buried.

"Arthur gave me a key," Van Helsing said. He opened the door of the tomb and let Dr. Seward go inside first.

The flowers that had brightened the tomb were now wilted and dead. Spiders and beetles had made it their home. Dust covered everything.

They found Lucy's coffin among the others of her family. Van Helsing took a screwdriver from his bag.

"What are you going to do?" Dr. Seward asked.

"Open her coffin. It is the proof I spoke of."

He unscrewed the lid and removed it. Inside was a sealed casing of lead. Van Helsing began to make a hole in it. Dr. Seward drew back. He was afraid of the smell that would come from the dead body.

But Van Helsing held his candle down near the opening. Dr. Seward looked inside. The coffin was empty!

Dr. Seward was shocked, but the professor

did not seem surprised at all.

"Why do you think the body is absent?" Van Helsing asked.

"Grave robbers," Dr. Seward guessed. "They stole it. What else could it be?"

Van Helsing screwed the lid of the coffin back in place.

"We will see," he said. "We must watch now. You take that side of the tomb. I'll hide over here. Keep your eyes open."

A distant clock struck twelve as the two men waited. It struck one and then two. Dr. Seward was chilled to the bone.

Suddenly, though, he saw a white streak moving through the graveyard. It wove among the shadows of the trees. Dr. Seward hurried across to get a closer look. He tripped over a fallen gravestone. Then he saw the white figure again. It flashed toward the tomb and disappeared.

When he met Van Helsing, the professor was holding a small sleeping child.

"Are you satisfied?" Van Helsing asked.

They Used the Key to Open Lucy's Tomb.

"No," Dr. Seward said. "What did I see?"

"Look at this child," Van Helsing said. He struck a match.

Dr. Seward examined the little boy's throat. It bore no mark, no puncture wound.

"We were just in time," Van Helsing said. They took the child to a place where a policeman would come. When they heard one approach, they placed the little boy in the pathway and went on.

"Tomorrow," Van Helsing told his friend, "you will have your real proof."

The next day they went out to the graveyard in the afternoon. All the funerals were over for the day. They were alone. Again they used the key to open Lucy's tomb.

"What is the point of this?" Dr. Seward asked. "We know the tomb is empty."

"Wait and see," Van Helsing said. He unscrewed the lid of the coffin.

Dr. Seward was again shocked. There lay Lucy, looking more beautiful than ever. Her lips were red, her cheeks rosy.

"But the teeth," Van Helsing said. He pulled back Lucy's lips. "They are longer and sharper than before. It is with these teeth that she has been attacking the little children."

"This leaves me completely baffled," Dr. Seward said. "What can possibly explain it?"

"She is one of the Un-Dead," Van Helsing said. "She was bitten by a vampire and has become one of them. We must kill her in her sleep. We will ask Arthur and his friend Quincey to help. It will be an awful task. But we must do it."

They left the graveyard and went home.

The next day Dr. Seward and Van Helsing met with Arthur and Quincey.

"We are going to need as much help as possible in what we do," Van Helsing said to Arthur. "Because you loved Miss Lucy, I ask you to come along. But it will be a difficult task."

"What are you talking about?" Arthur asked.

"We can do no harm to Miss Lucy now, because she is dead. But what if she is not

"She Is One of the Un-Dead."

really dead?"

"What do you mean?" Arthur cried, jumping to his feet. "Was she buried alive?"

"No, she is one of the Un-Dead," Van Helsing said. "We have a duty to her now. We must free her soul."

"How can we do that?"

"You will see. First you must see proof, as Dr. Seward here has seen proof. You must see with your own eyes."

The four men met at the graveyard that night. Dark clouds obscured the moon but now and then they let flashes of light through. The men came to the tomb.

"We were here yesterday and found Lucy in her coffin," Van Helsing. "Isn't that so, Dr. Seward?"

"Yes, that's true."

They entered and Van Helsing opened the coffin.

"Tell me, what do you see?" he asked.

The coffin was empty!

"Where is she?" Arthur demanded. "What

have you done with her body?"

"Nothing," Van Helsing said. "You will see for yourself."

The men went back outside. The night air seemed fresh and healthy after the damp smell of the tomb. Van Helsing closed the door of the tomb and placed garlic all around it.

"Now we wait," he said.

They hid in the graveyard and waited, each man afraid of what he might see. Then, through the dark, it came. A white figure, a woman. In her arms she held a sleeping child. Arthur started to move, but Van Helsing held him back.

The figure came closer. The moon broke through the clouds. In its light, they could see the face of the white figure. It was Lucy!

The four men moved in front of the door of the tomb. Van Helsing shined the light of his lantern on the woman who approached them. All of their hearts grew as cold as ice.

It was Lucy, all right. But her sweetness had turned to cruelty. She drew back and snarled

She Flung the Child to the Ground.

at them. Her lips were red with fresh blood. Blood trickled down her chin and onto her gown. Her eyes were red and furious.

She took the child and flung it to the ground, growling the way a dog growls. The child gave a cry and lay there moaning.

Lucy's lips curled back in a hideous smile. "Come to me, Arthur," she said. "Come so that we may rest together. Come, my husband, come."

Her voice was as sweet as it had been in life. Arthur opened his arms and took a step toward her. Van Helsing sprang forward and held out a gold crucifix.

Lucy recoiled. She ran past him toward the tomb. But the garlic repelled her. She turned and stared at the men with a look of awful hatred. Her eyes sparkled. Her brow wrinkled. Her blood-stained mouth opened wide. It was a look meant to kill.

"Do you believe me now?" Van Helsing asked Arthur and Quincey. "Do you see what she has become?"

"Yes," they agreed. "We will do what you say."

The professor took the garlic from around the tomb. Lucy slipped through a crack, passing inside the grave without even opening the door.

"We will meet back here tomorrow afternoon," Van Helsing said. "We will do what we must to give her rest."

The three young men, Arthur, Quincey Morris, and Dr. Seward met the next afternoon with Professor Van Helsing. They noticed that he was carrying a long leather sack, not his usual medical bag.

They went to the tomb and entered. Van Helsing unscrewed the lid of Lucy's coffin. There she lay.

"She's as beautiful as ever," Arthur said. "Is it really her, Professor, or a demon that has taken her shape?"

"It is her body, but it is not her," he answered. He pointed to the sharp teeth and the blood stains. "We must all get to work

"Is It Really Her?"

immediately, my friend."

From his bag, the professor took a set of operating knives. He laid them on another coffin. Then he drew out a stake, three feet long and three inches thick. It was sharpened at one end and hardened by fire. He also took a heavy hammer.

"The Un-Dead can never truly die," he said. "They must prey on others, turning them also into Un-Dead. If Lucy had kissed you, Arthur, you too would have become Un-Dead. The children whose blood she sucks are not lost yet. But in time they will come under her spell. We must make sure she dies in truth. Then her soul will be set free."

"Let me be the one to do it," Arthur said. "Tell me how. I will not weaken."

"It will be an awful task," Van Helsing said. "This stake must be driven through her body. Then we will cut off her head."

Arthur trembled as he took up the thick stake. He placed the sharp point directly over Lucy's heart. Van Helsing began to read a prayer for the dead. Arthur lifted the hammer high and brought it down, striking with all his might.

The Thing in the coffin writhed. A hideous, blood-curdling screech came from the red lips. The body shook and twisted. The teeth clamped together.

Arthur did not hesitate. He drove the stake deeper and deeper. Blood spurted all around. Then the body stopped trembling and became calm. It was over.

The hammer dropped from Arthur's hand and he fell backward. The deed had been a terrible strain on him.

"But look, Arthur," Van Helsing said. "Look at her now."

There in the coffin lay Lucy as she had been in life. She was no longer a vampire. A calm light washed over her delicate face.

"Thank you, Professor," Arthur said. "I know she is truly at peace now."

The men sawed off the end of the stake. They cut off the corpse's head and filled the mouth

"Once We Begin, We Cannot Stop."

with garlic, as Van Helsing instructed. Finally, they replaced the lid of the coffin and left the tomb.

"One step of our work is done," Van Helsing said. "A greater task remains. We must find the vampire, Count Dracula, and stamp him out. Are you men ready for this difficult and dangerous business?"

"Yes," they all agreed.

"And will you follow it to the end no matter what?"

Again they said they would.

"We will meet tomorrow to make our plans. Once we begin, we cannot stop."

CHAPTER 13

Vampires!

Mina and Jonathan traveled to London as they had promised. There they stayed with Dr. Seward in his house on the grounds of the insane asylum. That night they met with the Doctor and with Arthur Holmwood and Quincey Morris. Professor Van Helsing brought them all together to talk about what needed to be done.

"We must look at the facts that may help us track down Count Dracula," he said. "We have an awful task before us: to rid the earth of this

They Stayed with Dr. Seward.

awful monster. We need all the knowledge and all the help we can get."

They gathered together diaries, letters, newspaper articles, anything that might give clues to Count Dracula's actions in England. Mina began to examine everything and put all the facts in order.

"First," Van Helsing said, "I must tell all of you something about the enemy we will be fighting. Perhaps it will be hard for some of you to believe, but you must know everything."

Vampires exist, Van Helsing told them. They are the Un-Dead, persons who never die. They are each stronger than twenty men. They are very smart. Their cleverness has grown over centuries. They cast no shadow in the light and when they stand before a mirror, they have no reflection.

What can they do? They can create storms and produce fog. They can command animals like owls and rats and wolves. They can turn into wolves or bats or whatever animal they want. They can see in the dark. They can become small enough to slip through a tiny crack. They can vanish into thin air.

"They are an awfully powerful enemy," Arthur said. "What if we fail to defeat them?"

"It is not just a matter of life and death," Van Helsing answered. "If we fail, we will become like them. We will become foul things of the night. We will forever walk the earth, sucking the blood of the living. Make no mistake, my friends, this is a terribly serious battle we are fighting. I am old, I have less time to lose. Do you who are young dare join me?"

All of them said they would do everything possible to hunt down Dracula. They joined hands and vowed to work together until the vampire was destroyed.

"Have courage," Van Helsing said. "Together we are strong. We can act freely day and night. Vampires are not so free."

"Do you mean they have some weaknesses?" Quincey Morris asked.

"Yes," Van Helsing said. "First, they must have blood. Vampires do not eat regular food as

"It Is Blood They Want."

we do. Jonathan never saw Count Dracula eat or drink. It is blood they want. When they suck the blood of the living they grow strong. They even become younger. But without this blood, they weaken.

"A vampire has other limits. He can only enter a house if someone inside invites him in. Afterwards, though, he can come into that house at any time.

"His power is of the night. When day comes, he loses his power and must rest. He must live in a coffin that contains earth from his native country. That is why Dracula had to have the boxes of dirt from Transylvania.

"He can only change himself into another form at sunrise, noon, or sunset, no other time. He can only pass over water with the help of others, or when the tide is full.

"Most important," Van Helsing told them, "are the things that take away his power. Garlic is one. Also sacred symbols like the crucifix. Driving a stake through his heart and cutting off his head are the ways to kill him so that he becomes truly dead, never to rise again."

"But who is Dracula really?" Jonathan asked the professor.

"The Dracula family is a very old one in Transylvania," Van Helsing explained. "Count Dracula was a great warrior who fought against the invasion of the Turks. But he practiced black magic and he slipped into the hands of the devil."

Suddenly they were all startled by a pistol shot that crashed through the window.

"What was that?" Arthur cried.

Dr. Seward jumped up and ran to the window. Outside he saw Quincey Morris. No one had noticed when he had quietly gotten up and left the room.

"Sorry about that," Quincey said. "I went outside because I saw a very large bat hovering at the window. I hate the horrid things."

"Did you hit it?" Arthur asked him.

"I don't think I did. It flew away into the woods, over toward Carfax."

Quincey came back in and they continued

A Pistol Shot Through the Window

talking about ways of tracking down Dracula.

"I've found something interesting in these records," Mina said. "Fifty boxes of earth that were taken from the ship in Whitby. Do you know where they were shipped to? To Carfax estate, right next door!"

All the men were impressed by this information.

"So Dracula has been living close by," Arthur said.

"Maybe that explains the strange behavior of Renfield," Dr. Seward said.

"Tell us about it," Van Helsing said.

"At times he acts sane and reasonable. Other times he becomes wild. Several times he escaped and ran over to Carfax. He often called out, 'Master!' Once he attacked several workman who were removing packages from Carfax."

"What type of packages?" Van Helsing asked.

"Big boxes shaped like coffins."

"Do you know what that means?" asked the

professor.

"I'm afraid so," Dr. Seward said. "It means that Count Dracula is preparing other places around London to hide. It means that our job of finding him will be much more difficult."

"The first thing we should do," Arthur said, "is to go over to Carfax and see how many boxes are left there."

"Certainly," Van Helsing said. "We must go tonight. But it is we men who will do it. Miss Mina should stay behind."

"I think I should go along," Mina said. "I'm just as ready to hunt vampires as any man." But the men wouldn't hear of it.

"You stay behind, darling," Jonathan told his wife. "You'll be safe here."

As the men were preparing to go over and search the estate, one of the asylum guards ran in and told Dr. Seward that the patient Renfield urgently wanted to see him.

"I think we should see what he wants," Dr. Seward told the others. "He may give us clues to the movements of the Count."

"Let Me Leave Here," Renfield Said.

All of the men went down to Renfield's room. Dr. Seward introduced the others to his patient, who was sitting calmly on his bed.

"Arthur Holmwood," Renfield said. "I knew your father. I was sorry to hear of his death. Mr. Quincey Morris, I understand you come from Texas. You should be proud to call such a great state home. And Professor Van Helsing, what an honor to meet a famous scientist like you. I have read all of your books."

The others looked at Dr. Seward curiously. This man did not seem like a lunatic. He seemed completely normal. But Dr. Seward remembered other times when Renfield had acted sane one minute and then suddenly turned into a madman.

"What was it you wanted?" Dr. Seward asked Renfield.

"I wanted to ask you to let me leave here," Renfield said. "As you can see, I am no longer insane. There is no reason to keep me locked up."

"Maybe it's something we can consider

later," Dr. Seward said.

"No, I mean tonight, right away," Renfield said. "It's terribly important that I do not stay here a second longer. I ask you this not just for myself. It is important for a much larger reason."

"What is that?" Dr. Seward asked.

"I can't tell you."

"I don't think it would be wise for you to leave us just yet," Dr. Seward told him.

Renfield became excited. "Please, Doctor," he said. "I beg you. Send guards with me if you must. Put me in a straitjacket. But let me leave this place. I am not insane now. Can't you see that? I am a man fighting for his soul."

"I'm sorry," Dr. Seward said. "We must go. Try to behave yourself."

"You are making a mistake," Renfield shouted. "An awful mistake. You'll see!"

The men left Renfield's room. They finished their preparations and set out for the dark and mysterious estate next door.

"An Awful Mistake!"

CHAPTER 14

A Terrible Accident

"My friends, we are going to a terribly dangerous place," Professor Van Helsing warned his friends. "Our enemy is very powerful. He can easily break a man's neck. We can do nothing to hurt him in the ordinary way. We must guard ourselves against his touch."

He handed each of the men a little silver crucifix and a wreath of garlic blossoms.

"Keep this near your heart," he said, "and put these flowers around your neck."

They also brought with them a revolver,

some flashlights, and a set of skeleton keys. When they arrived at the door of the big house at Carfax, Dr. Seward tried several keys. He finally found one that opened the lock.

"Check the latch on that door," Arthur suggested. "We don't want to be locked in. We may have to get out in a hurry."

The floor was coated with several inches of dust. There were tangles of spiders' webs everywhere. They found a ring of keys on a table.

Jonathan had studied maps of the estate when he was helping Count Dracula to purchase it. He led them to a solid oak door with iron bands that closed off the old chapel. They used one of the keys to open it.

"Phew!" Quincey Morris said. "What is that awful stink?"

The smell inside was terrible. The closed room had all the stench of death, along with the pungent, sharp smell of fresh blood. It made the men sick to breathe the foul air. All of them drew back, ready to run outside. But

. . . The Evil Eyes and Lips of Dracula . . .

they had no choice. They had to continue into that sickening place.

Their first task was to count the boxes of earth that rested on the floor of the chapel. There were twenty-nine there. That meant that almost half of them had already been moved out.

"We must search this place for any clue about where the other boxes have gone," Van Helsing said.

They split up and began to examine every corner and crevice of the chapel. Once, Jonathan thought he saw a pale, familiar face—the evil red eyes and red lips of Count Dracula. But in an instant the face disappeared.

Quincey Morris heard a rustling sound on the floor. He shined his flashlight down and saw rats.

"They're everywhere!" he whispered to the others.

From all around came hundreds and hundreds of crawling, gnawing rats.

"I thought they might be a problem," Arthur said. "I came prepared." He took out a silver whistle and blew it.

From next door, three terrier dogs came running over. At first they wouldn't enter. They only stood at the door and howled. But once Arthur lifted them over the doorway, they went to work. They chased the rats around, grabbing them in their jaws and killing as many as they could. Once they were done clearing the chapel, the whole place seemed fresher, as if an evil presence had departed.

The men continued on, searching the main house. They found nothing that would tell them where Count Dracula might be hiding. When they finished, dawn was already breaking in the east. They returned to their rooms at Dr. Seward's.

Jonathan noted that Mina was a little paler than usual. He hoped she hadn't been too worried about his safety.

They all slept late after their ordeal. Even Mina seemed to feel the strain. She was still

Three Terrier Dogs Came Running.

sleeping after Jonathan got up. When he called her, she looked at him for a moment as if she didn't recognize him. It was a look almost of terror.

"How are you feeling, my dear?" Jonathan asked.

"I was troubled all night," she said. "First I saw an odd steak of white mist moving toward the house. Then that patient downstairs, Mr. Renfield, began to make noise. I could hear him arguing with someone, but I couldn't understand the words. Then he seemed to be fighting. I was so frightened that I crept into bed and pulled the covers over my head. I must have had bad dreams because I'm more tired than if I had not slept at all."

"You have been worrying too much about this business with Count Dracula," her husband said. "We won't say another word to you about it."

"I think you should," she said. "It was a mistake to leave me out. I'm sure of it."

That morning Van Helsing went down to see

the patient Renfield again. Renfield was acting very differently than he had the night before. He sat sullenly on his bed and would not talk, only to call Van Helsing a "silly Dutchman." The patient had even gone back to his old ways. He was again spreading sugar on his window sill to attract flies. The ones he caught he immediately ate.

He certainly is insane, Van Helsing said. Dr. Seward is right to keep him locked up.

Jonathan and the others went out to try and find what had become of the twenty-one boxes of earth that Dracula had already moved from his estate. Jonathan talked to one of the workmen who had helped move the boxes.

"We delivered them to a house in the center of London, in Piccadilly," he said. "A skinny old man was there to let us in. In fact, he even helped us move the boxes. He was so strong I couldn't believe it. Carried those big boxes of dirt as if they weighed nothing at all."

After Jonathan reported this to the others, Van Helsing said, "The Count is very smart. As

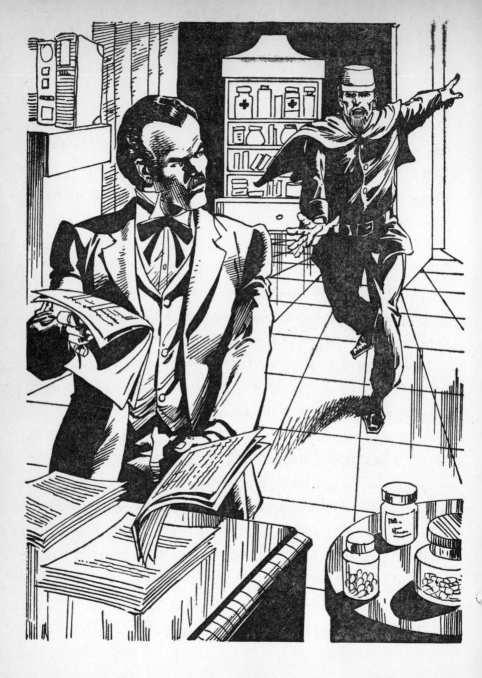

A Terrible Accident

long as he has a box of his native soil to hide in, we will not be able to find him. We must find this house in Piccadilly before he has a chance to move the boxes to even more places. We must place garlic on all the boxes during daylight. That is when Dracula is weakest. That is when we must destroy his refuge."

That night, Dr. Seward went in to look at Mina. Jonathan was a little worried because his wife seemed tired and weak. He was afraid the strain of vampire hunting was making her ill. Dr. Seward noticed how pale she had become.

"You must eat better and try to get more rest," he said. "You've been working too hard, arranging all the documents about the case."

He left her and Jonathan so they could get a good night's sleep. While he was working in his office, one of the guards from the asylum came pounding on Dr. Seward's door.

"Come quick, Doctor!" he cried. "It's Renfield. He's had a terrible accident."

CHAPTER 15

Mina in Danger

When Dr. Seward reached Renfield's room he found the patient lying on the floor in a glittering pool of blood. It was clear Renfield had received some terrible injuries. His face was bruised as if it had been beaten against the floor.

"I think his back is broken," the guard said. "He can't move his right arm or leg. He's been hurt very badly."

"Help me to put him back on his bed," Dr. Seward said.

Renfield Had Terrible Injuries.

They lifted Renfield carefully. "Run and tell Dr. Van Helsing to come here at once. Hurry!" Dr. Seward said.

Van Helsing came and examined the patient. "We must operate soon or he will die," he said.

They sent the guard away. They didn't want him to hear what Renfield might say if he woke up.

"His skull is broken," Van Helsing said. "After the operation he might be able to talk. It is important that we find out what happened to the poor man."

A minute later, Arthur and Quincey came running into the room. "We couldn't sleep," Arthur said. "What happened to poor Renfield?"

"I hope we will find out," Van Helsing said. He prepared to operate on Renfield's head. "The patient is barely breathing. He might die at any moment. There is no time to lose. His words may save many lives."

When the operation was done, all four men waited for Renfield to awaken. Suddenly the patient opened his eyes and looked around wildly.

"Where am I?" he said. "I've had a terrible dream. What's wrong with my face? Why can't I move?"

"Tell us your dream," Van Helsing said.

"Dr. Van Helsing, how good of you to be here," Renfield said. Again he seemed completely normal. "I know that it was no dream. What I remember really happened. Now I only have a few minutes before I die—or worse."

"Tell us what happened," Van Helsing asked him again.

"It began that night when I begged you to let me go. I wanted to explain, but I couldn't speak about it. After you left, he came to the window in a mist."

"Who came?" Dr. Seward asked.

"Who? Dracula! He was laughing with his red mouth and sharp white teeth. He wanted me to ask him to come in, but I wouldn't at first. But he promised me things."

"What did he promise?" Van Helsing asked.

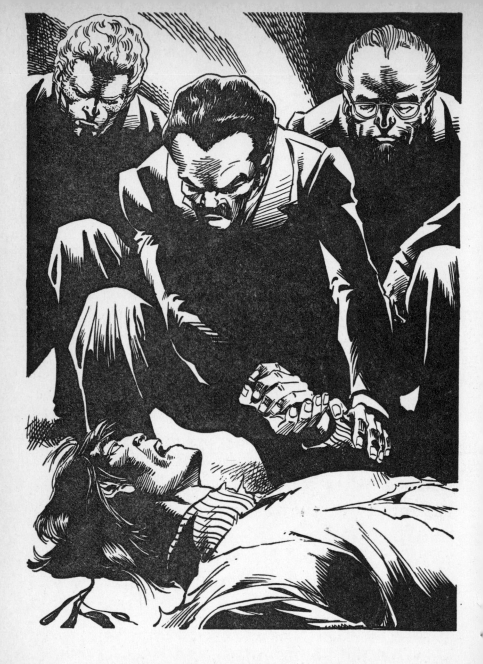

"... Taking the Life out of Her."

"Life," Renfield murmured. "He said I could have all the flies I wanted, big fat ones. And spiders. And rats. Rats, rats, rats! he said. Hundreds and thousands of them. All full of red blood, full of life. He showed me the yard outside teeming with rats, all their little eyes glowing red like his."

"So you let him in?" Dr. Seward asked.

Renfield struggled to speak. "I couldn't help it. I opened the window and said, 'Come in, Master.' He was inside in an instant. Then, all day I waited for him to send me the rats. But he didn't. He began to come every night, without even knocking, as if he owned the place. He sneered at me."

"Why did he come?" Van Helsing asked. He could see the patient was near death.

"Why?" Renfield said. "For Mrs. Harker. I saw her today. She is not the same. She is pale, as if all her blood has run out. Dracula has been taking the life out of her."

All the men became tense. They suddenly realized the danger that Mina was in.

"When he came tonight, I was ready," Renfield went on. "I grabbed him. You know madmen have unusual strength. I used all my power to hold him. I would not let him get to her again. I thought I could beat him. But then I saw his eyes. They burned at me and made me weak. He lifted me up and flung me onto the floor over and over. Everything went dark. The last thing I remember is a mist seeping under the door."

"This is the worst yet," Van Helsing said. "He is here now. And we know why. It may not be too late. But we must hurry. Every second matters."

The four men ran back to their rooms and gathered their crucifixes and garlic flowers. They met in the hallway outside of the room where Mina and Jonathan slept.

"Should we disturb them at this late hour?" Quincey Morris asked.

"We must," Van Helsing said. "If the door is locked we will break it in."

Van Helsing tried the door. It was locked. Dr.

"Every Second Matters."

Seward and the others threw themselves against it. It burst open and they fell into the room. What they saw made the hair stand up on their heads and their hearts seem to stop.

In the moonlight by the window, Jonathan lay in a stupor. Mina was kneeling on the edge of the bed, her nightdress smeared with blood. By her side stood a figure all dressed in black. Dracula! He clutched both her hands in his powerful hand. With his other hand he held her by the back of the neck.

Dracula turned toward them, his eyes red with hatred. His sharp teeth clacked together like those of a wild animal. He threw Mina roughly back onto the bed and leaped toward the men.

At the same moment, all of them held up their crucifixes. The Count stopped dead. They came toward him, the crosses held out. As a cloud blotted out the moonlight for an instant, Dracula suddenly vanished. The men saw a mist slide under the door and that was all.

Mina let out a terrifying scream. She lay on

the bed, ghostly pale, her lips and cheeks and chin all smeared with blood. Her eyes were mad with terror. Her hands still bore the marks of Dracula's powerful grip.

Dr. Seward put her in bed and covered her up. Arthur and Quincey ran after the Count.

A minute later Jonathan recovered from his faint.

"What has happened?" he asked. "What is wrong with Mina? What does all this blood mean? Can't you help her?"

Gradually, he remembered what had happened. He pulled on his coat and said, "Dr. Van Helsing and Dr. Seward, guard her while I go out and look for him."

"No, Jonathan," Mina cried. "I have suffered enough tonight. Don't leave me!"

Jonathan went over to hug his wife. But when she saw the blood that she left on his shirt, from her mouth and from the two holes in her throat, she shrank back.

"No! I must never touch you again," she said. "I am unclean. Unclean!"

. . . White Mist Seeping Under the Door . . .

Arthur and Quincey returned from their searches. Arthur said that the Count had found their records of his movements and burned them. He didn't know that Mina had made another copy and placed it in the safe. Arthur had checked Renfield's room. The poor man was dead.

Quincey reported that he'd seen a bat fly from Renfield's window. He said, "I expected him to go back to Carfax and thought I would get a shot at him. But he headed in another direction, toward one of his other hiding places."

Van Helsing turned to Mina. "Now, my dear, you must tell us exactly what happened."

"I took the pill that you gave me to help me sleep," she said. "But I still didn't feel drowsy. I was afraid of the dreams that might come if I dozed off. But I must have finally fallen asleep. When I awoke, Jonathan was asleep beside me and the moonlight was coming in the window. I noticed a white mist seeping under the door and it made me afraid."

"Why didn't you wake me, dear?" Jonathan asked.

"I tried, but you wouldn't wake up. Suddenly, the mist became a man, a tall, thin man standing by my bed. He was dressed in black, but his skin was all white. His sharp teeth showed between the red lips. I knew who he was."

"You couldn't call out for help?" Van Helsing asked.

"I wanted to," Mina said. "But the man told me he would kill Jonathan if I made a sound. He whispered to me, 'I am thirsty, very thirsty.' And then he leaned over my throat."

She buried her face in her hands and sobbed. Jonathan groaned. Mina pulled herself together and went on. "My strength faded away. Finally he said, 'You have helped those men hunt me. Now I will make you my companion and helper, just like your friend Lucy. When I command, you will obey.' "

"What happened then?" Van Helsing asked her.

"He opened a vein in his chest with his sharp

"I Knew Who He Was."

nails," Mina said. "He pressed my mouth to the wound. I had to suffocate or else swallow...Oh, what have I done? Why has this happened to me?"

"We were wrong to leave Miss Mina out," Van Helsing said. "See what has happened. From now on, she will help us hunt Dracula, too."

They all agreed that this would be best.

"And if I see any signs that I am becoming a vampire myself," Mina said, "if I might harm those I love, I will die first. I will kill myself."

"No!" Van Helsing shouted. "You must not die. If you die you will become as he is, Un-Dead. You must struggle to live. Dracula is the one who must die. He must die for all time. We must find him and drive the stake through his heart. It is the only hope for Miss Mina, the only hope for all of us."

CHAPTER 16

On Dracula's Trail

In the morning, they all met again to plan their hunt for the vampire. First, Arthur and Quincey reported on their search for the Count's houses.

"From our investigations, we found three," Arthur said. "The first you know about. It's in Piccadilly, right in the center of London. The other two are on quiet streets in other parts of the city."

"The key," Professor Van Helsing said, "is that house in Piccadilly. That was the first one

"We Will Be Waiting for Him."

he moved the boxes to. That is a good place for him. He can come and go and mix with all the people there. If we can get into that house, we may be able to trap the Count."

"It's a good thing," Dr. Seward said, "that we did not disturb the boxes next door at Carfax. The Count still doesn't know how close we are on his trail. We have time to track him down."

"Yes," Van Helsing said. "We will go to all the houses and put garlic on the boxes so that Dracula can never use them again. I suspect that he may come back to the house in Piccadilly sometime during the day. He will need to rest. We will be there waiting for him."

"What about the boxes in Carfax?" Arthur asked.

"We will put garlic on those before we leave," Van Helsing said. "Then if he returns here he will not be able to stay."

But Jonathan said that he couldn't go along. He had to stay and protect Mina.

"No, you must go," Mina told him. "They will need every man to trap Dracula. You know more of the Count's business than anyone. You are the only one who has talked with him. As a lawyer, you can help the others get inside the house in Piccadilly. It is far more important to destroy Dracula than to stay here in order to guard me."

Jonathan agreed she was right. Before they left, Van Helsing examined Mina carefully. She was pale, but her teeth had not yet begun to grow sharp. There was time to save her, but they would have to hurry.

"You will be safe here, Miss Mina," he said. "Dracula can do you no harm until sunset. We will return before that. But to be sure, I will leave you this crucifix."

He took a gold cross and touched it to Mina's forehead. She let out an awful scream. Where the metal touched her flesh, it burned it as if it had been white-hot!

Mina instantly understood that it meant she was beginning to turn into a vampire. If they weren't able to find Dracula, she would spend eternity wandering the earth with the Undead.

There Was Time to Save Her.

She cried out in terror.

"You may have to bear that scar on your forehead until we can find the vampire and destroy him," Van Helsing said. "But I assure you, we will succeed. We will not fail you."

As they were leaving, Jonathan secretly vowed that if Mina had to be a vampire, he too would become one. He would not leave her alone, even if it meant giving up his own soul.

The men crossed over to the Carfax estate and entered the ruined chapel. There they found the same boxes of earth they'd seen on their last visit. This time, they placed garlic flowers and a crucifix on top of each box. Now, if Dracula returned, he would have nowhere to hide and nowhere to rest.

"That is well done," Van Helsing said. "If we are lucky, Dracula will be dead by sundown."

They all took horse-drawn cabs to Piccadilly. There Arthur and Jonathan hired a locksmith to open the door of the house that Dracula had bought.

A foul smell filled the house. In the dining

room they found the boxes.

"Twenty-one boxes came here," Van Helsing said. "You discovered that twelve boxes have been moved to the Count's other two houses. That means there should be nine left."

"But there are only eight here," Dr. Seward said. "He must have hidden the last one somewhere else."

"Still, we are closing in on him," Van Helsing said. "Here are keys to his other houses. Quincey, you and Arthur take them and go put garlic and crosses on those boxes. I will wait here with Dr. Seward and Jonathan. The Count may arrive at any time."

While they waited, Dr. Seward studied Jonathan's face. A few days before he had been a young man. Now his hair was white and his face haggard. It was terrible for him to think of the fate that lay in store for his lovely wife.

Van Helsing tried to cheer up his friends. "Today is our day!" he said. "We will not let Dracula escape."

The house was very quiet. Suddenly, a knock

The Three Men Moved Forward.

came on the front door. Van Helsing motioned for silence and opened it. It was a telegraph boy. He handed the professor a message.

"What does it say?" Jonathan asked.

"It is from your dear wife," Van Helsing replied. "She says Dracula came back to Carfax but hurried away again immediately."

"Then we shall soon meet!" Jonathan said. "Good!"

Another knock sounded at the door. The three men moved forward. Each had a pistol or a knife in one hand, a crucifix in the other.

This time it was Arthur and Quincey returning.

"We found the other two houses," Arthur said. "Six boxes in each. We made them useless for the vampire."

"Excellent," the professor said. "We must now wait. But if it grows too late we will have to hurry back to Miss Mina. We cannot leave her alone after dark."

But even as he spoke the men heard a key quietly turning in the front door. They retreated to the dining room. Quincey Morris, who was used to organizing hunting expeditions, took charge. He made a quick plan of attack. Professor Van Helsing, Dr. Seward, and Jonathan stood behind the door. Arthur and Quincey hid near the window, ready to block that exit.

The men waited nervously as slow careful steps came nearer along the hallway. Perhaps the Count suspected some surprise.

Suddenly, Dracula burst into the room with a leap. Jonathan immediately threw himself in front of the door so that he could not escape.

Dracula stared at the men with a low snarl and a look of cold anger. He bared his long and pointed teeth. The men all stepped closer, each holding a crucifix in his hand. Jonathan suddenly lunged forward, striking at the Count with his long knife!

Dracula was quick. He jumped back to keep the blade from piercing his heart. Instead, it only tore his coat, letting a stream of gold coins fall to the floor.

Suddenly, Dracula Burst into the Room.

The hate in the Count's eyes was awful to see. His pale skin turned yellow-green. As Jonathan raised his knife once more to strike, Dracula slid under his arm and dashed across the room. He threw himself at the window and crashed through, falling into the yard outside.

The men all ran to the window. They looked to where the Count was standing, unhurt.

"You think you can harm me?" he said, "You'll be sorry, all of you. My revenge has just begun. You'll see!"

He turned and hurried across the yard to the stable. He went through the stable door and was gone.

Arthur and Quincey rushed outside. Jonathan even lowered himself from the window. But Dracula had barred the stable door. When they finally opened it, he was gone.

"Hurry," Van Helsing told the others. "We must get back to Miss Mina before the sun sets. Our efforts were good, but not good enough. Dracula is more dangerous than ever!"

CHAPTER 17

Back to Transylvania

"He fears us," Van Helsing told the others as they returned to Dr. Seward's. "He was in a great hurry to escape. This is a good sign. Now he only has one box of earth left, one place to hide. When we find that, we can destroy him forever."

When they arrived they told Mina all that had happened.

"I can't wait to drive the stake into that monster!" Jonathan said. "I would give anything to do it now."

"There Is Someone in the Hallway."

"You must remember though, dear," Mina said, "that Count Dracula is also a tortured soul. It is certain that you will have to put him at rest as you did poor Lucy. But you should have pity on him."

"I will never pity that fiend," Jonathan said. "I will send his soul to hell first."

"Don't say that," she pleaded. "Remember that I, too, may need such pity someday. I only hope that someone will help free my soul."

Jonathan wept to hear his wife talk this way. He had forgotten that she, too, could become a vampire like Dracula. He asked her to forgive him.

During the night Mina awoke in terror. "Jonathan," she whispered, "there is someone in the hallway."

Jonathan took up his big knife and crept to the door. When he eased it open, he saw Quincey Morris sitting outside.

"One of us will be on watch here all night," Quincey told him. "Just in case Dracula decides to return."

Jonathan told Mina and she was able to sleep peacefully until just before dawn. But then she awoke again and told Jonathan to go get Dr. Van Helsing right away.

When the professor came, she asked him to hypnotize her. "I feel that I can speak freely as the sun comes up," she said. "But hurry, time is short."

Professor Van Helsing was able to put Mina into a trance quickly. He suspected that now she would be in contact with the Count. He motioned for Jonathan to bring in the others so that they could hear.

"Where are you?" Van Helsing asked her.

"I don't know, everything is dark."

"Do you hear anything?"

"Yes," she said. "I hear water lapping. I hear footsteps, men moving, a chain clanking."

The sun was completely up now. Mina lay back on her pillow. Then she awoke and asked, "Have I been talking in my sleep?"

"You told us a great deal," Van Helsing said. "The Count is on a ship. The clanking of the

In a Trance

chain is the anchor being pulled in. That means the ship is sailing away."

"He's leaving London," Arthur said.

"Yes," Van Helsing agreed. "This is an important clue. We knew he was trying to escape us, and now he has succeeded. We must now begin to plan how to follow him."

"Why follow him at all?" Jonathan asked. "He's gone now. Let him go."

"Why?" Van Helsing said, very serious. "Because if we do not find him and destroy him, Miss Mina will become as he is. We must do it for her sake. We cannot fail."

During the day Professor Van Helsing went out to investigate along with Quincey and Arthur. They knew the Count would want to return to Transylvania, so they looked for a ship that was bound for the Black Sea. They found one, the *Czarina Catherine*. It had sailed that morning.

The men went to the wharf where the ship had been docked. They found a man in the office on the pier. "Yes," he said, "I remember. A tall, thin man dressed in black came and wanted to put a box on that ship. He sent the box over. Then, just before the ship sailed, he came again. He said he wanted to see how his box was stowed. He went on the ship and they showed it to him. Then a fog came in, but it lifted in time for the ship to set sail."

That night, they reported back to the others.

"The ship is headed for Varna, on the Black Sea," Van Helsing said. "That means we have time. We can get there much more quickly by train."

"What will we do when we arrive?" Quincey asked. "Call the police?"

"No," the professor said, "this is no job for the police. We must do it our own way. We must get aboard the ship before Dracula can escape. That is our only hope."

The next day they began to make plans to travel to the Black Sea. During a quiet moment, Van Helsing took Dr. Seward aside.

"My friend John," he said, "I know that you

They Crossed the English Channel.

have noticed the same thing that I have. Miss Mina is changing. Her teeth are sharper now, her eyes more hard. And she is often silent. I am afraid that she is becoming a vampire more quickly than we thought."

"The Count must still have his power over her," Dr. Seward said. "That's why she can read Dracula's mind when you hypnotize her."

"We must be very careful. We must watch her very closely."

That night they met again. They made their final plans to take the train to Varna.

"The four of us will leave tomorrow," Van Helsing said. "Jonathan will stay behind to look after Mina."

"No," Mina said. "You must not leave me behind again. I am still under the power of the Count. I know it. If he calls me, I have to come to him. It's better that all of you be around to guard me. Besides, I can help by giving you clues about the Count's journey. Every morning you can hypnotize me and read Dracula's mind."

They all agreed that Mina was right, and that she should come along. Arthur and Quincey went to the station and bought tickets for all of them. The next day they crossed the English Channel and were headed for the Black Sea.

They arrived in Varna a few days later. They had plenty of time. The *Czarina Catherine* could not have reached the city ahead of them no matter how fast she sailed. Arthur arranged for messages to be sent to them about the progress of the ship wherever it was spotted. But every day the same message came, "No report of ship."

Every morning Professor Van Helsing hypnotized Mina. Every morning she reported the same thing as she entered the mind of the Count: "All is dark. I hear water rushing past."

So they knew the ship was still at sea, still moving toward Varna.

"When the ship arrives," Van Helsing told the others, "we must get aboard her before

"You Must Not Leave Me Behind Again."

sunset. Dracula will still be in his box. He can do nothing during the day. He will be at our mercy."

"We won't have any trouble with the officials," Arthur said. "In this country a bribe can buy anything."

They waited anxiously. To get aboard the ship when it docked, Arthur told the customs agents that something had been stolen from his friend in England and they thought it was in the box on the ship. As soon as the box was opened, Van Helsing and Dr. Seward would cut off Dracula's head and drive the stake through him. Jonathan, Quincey and Arthur would prevent anyone from interfering, using guns if necessary.

"Once the vampire's soul is free," Van Helsing told them, "his body will turn to dust. There will be no evidence left."

Finally, they got word. The *Czarina Catherine* was in the Black Sea. It would arrive in Varna in a day or two.

"Just in time," Van Helsing told Dr. Seward.

"Mina is getting worse. Perhaps it is because the Count is approaching."

The men spent the day preparing. Jonathan sharpened his long knife until it cut like a razor. Mina, though, grew weaker. In the morning they tried to hypnotize her as usual, but they were barely able to wake her. Her report was the same: the sound of water, nothing more.

Another day went by, and another.

"Where is that ship?" Jonathan asked.

"She may have been delayed by fog," Van Helsing said. "It's common on the Black Sea."

Another day passed and the ship still did not sail into Varna's harbor. But the following day Arthur received a telegram that brought them the news.

"*Czarina Catherine* has just docked at Galatz," it said.

"Galatz!" Van Helsing said. "That's hundreds of miles up the coast from here. Count Dracula has escaped again!"

The Telegram Stunned Everyone.

CHAPTER 18

Closing In

The telegram with news of the ship stunned everyone. They had been expecting that the Count would try some trick. They never thought that he could escape them completely.

Van Helsing immediately organized everyone to action. He sent Arthur to get train tickets to take them all to Galatz. Quincey and Jonathan would see the shipping officers to get permission to board the ship. Dr. Seward and Van Helsing himself would stay with Mina.

"It's strange, Professor," Mina told him. "I

feel the grip of the Count more loosely now."

"He is moving away from you," Van Helsing said. "He is not so concerned about keeping hold of you. He is anxious to escape us now. But there is still much danger. We must hurry to catch up with him."

Early the next morning they boarded the train for Galatz. As the sun came up, Van Helsing hypnotized Mina as usual.

"I still see darkness," she said. "The water is swirling softly now. I hear the creak of oars."

They hoped to reach Galatz before the Count had a chance to get far away. But the train ran late. They would not make it until after daybreak the next day.

That morning, too, the professor hypnotized Mina. Every day it was harder for her to read the Count's mind.

"I hear voices speaking in a strange language," she said this time. "And wolves howling."

They reached Galatz late in the morning. Arthur and Quincey took Mina to their hotel

"I Still See Darkness."

while Van Helsing, Dr. Seward, and Jonathan hurried to the wharf. They found Captain Donaldson, the commander of the *Czarina Catherine*.

"All the way from England," he said, "we had excellent weather. The wind was behind us the whole way. We had never made such good time. We entered the Black Sea and I expected to be in Varna ahead of schedule."

"What happened?" Van Helsing asked.

"We were overtaken by a bad fog," the captain told him. "We couldn't see where we were going. We just kept sailing on and on. Some of the crewmen started to get worried. They wanted to throw that box overboard. They didn't like the looks of the man who had brought it aboard. I told them we had no right to do so—it had to be delivered."

"So you brought the box here?" Dr. Seward asked.

"We kept sailing through the fog for five days," the captain said. "When it lifted, we found ourselves near Galatz. We pulled into the harbor. Just before the sun came up a man arrived who had orders to collect a box for Count Dracula. We were happy to give it to him."

"What was the man's name?" Jonathan demanded.

"Skinsky," the captain said. "Petrof Skinsky."

They went back into the town and asked some of the Romanians if they had ever heard of Petrof Skinsky.

One of them said, "Why, that's the man whose body they found yesterday in the churchyard. His throat had been torn open as if by a wild animal."

So Dracula really had escaped them. They had no idea where he was. That evening they all met to talk over their next step.

"I have been doing some reasoning," Mina said. "There are only three ways the Count could reach his castle—by road, by rail, or by water. He wouldn't go by road. We could catch up with him too easily. He wouldn't take a chance leaving his box of earth unattended on

"I'll Get Some Horses," Quincey Said.

a train. So he must have gone by water."

"Miss Mina makes a good point," Van Helsing said. "And when I hypnotized her she still heard the sound of water."

"There's more," Mina said. "How did the Count leave his castle? Remember, Jonathan told us the gypsies came for him. I think he has hired some gypsies to take him back. They will carry him up the river that leads to Borgo Pass. From there it's an easy trip up to Castle Dracula."

"Once more Miss Mina sees, where we are blind," the professor said. "But how can we catch the Count while he is still helpless?"

"I'll buy a steam boat," Arthur said. "I know how to operate one."

"And I'll get some horses," Quincey said. "I'll follow the river in case he lands anywhere along the way."

They decided that Jonathan should go with Arthur. The steam boat was likely to catch up with the gypsies the soonest. Because of Mina, Jonathan wanted to be the one to destroy

Dracula. Dr. Seward planned to ride with Quincey on the horses.

"And I will take Miss Mina by carriage right up to Castle Dracula," Van Helsing said.

"Not for all the world," Jonathan said. "She must stay away."

"No," the professor insisted. "She must come. If Dracula escapes us this time, it will not matter how far away she is. We need everyone's help. We need to get to his castle and make sure it is no refuge for him."

Jonathan agreed. They all prepared themselves. They took guns to shoot the wolves and crucifixes to ward off vampires. All except Mina. Her husband insisted that she take a pistol. But she could not touch a crucifix, since she was partly a vampire herself.

She Was Partly a Vampire Herself.

CHAPTER 19

The Final Battle

For three days they all moved up into the wild and mysterious mountains of Transylvania. Jonathan, on the puffing steam boat, worried about Mina. Quincey and Dr. Seward rode along the bank. They led extra horses so that the others might join them if they needed to.

Van Helsing and Mina drove along in a carriage, moving as fast as they could toward the Borgo Pass and the castle of Count Dracula. Once they stopped at an inn and a peasant woman saw the scar on Mina's forehead. She shrank back in terror. After that, Mina kept her hat on to hide the evil mark.

Arthur and Jonathan were almost at the point of catching the gypsies when their steamboat crashed in the rapids of the river. The gypsies were able to continue in their lighter craft. Arthur had to make some repairs quickly.

To make better time, Mina and Professor Van Helsing took turns driving. The country got wilder and wilder as they moved farther into the mountains. There were no more houses along the road. Everything was desolate.

Now Mina began to sleep so soundly all day that the professor could not waken her. He became very worried. The power of the vampire seemed to grow on her as they approached his castle. But they could not turn back.

When they reached the Borgo Pass, Mina pointed to a track leading to one side. "This is the way," she said.

"How do you know?" Van Helsing asked.

"Jonathan came this way when he first

He Made a Circle of Garlic Flowers.

approached Castle Dracula," she said.

Was that it? Or was the castle drawing Mina on now? The professor became even more worried. When they stopped and fixed dinner, Mina would not eat. She had no appetite. Another bad sign.

Finally they came in sight of Castle Dracula. It was very cold. Van Helsing decided to camp for the night. He made Mina a bed of the furs they had brought. Around it he made a circle of garlic flowers.

"Come closer to the fire, Miss Mina," he said.

She rose, but she did not come closer. "I can't," she said.

"Good. The circle will protect us. If you cannot move outside, they cannot move inside."

The horses screeched and tore at their ropes all night. Van Helsing had to go and calm them. When it was almost dawn and the fire started to die down, the snow came. It swirled all around them.

Through the flakes, Van Helsing saw three figures in white. At first he wasn't sure. But yes, they were three women. The same that Jonathan had seen at Castle Dracula. They came closer, closer, but could not come inside the ring of garlic.

They called out in sweet voices to Mina, "Come, sister. Come to us. Come!"

Van Helsing was glad to see that Mina looked on them with terror. She was not, yet, one of them. As the sun began to rise, the figures disappeared.

The gypsies had now transferred the box from their boat to a wagon. They were beginning to climb the long road toward Castle Dracula. Jonathan and Arthur left their steamboat behind and chased along on horses. Dr. Seward and Quincey Morris, riding by a different road, were also hurrying on.

Van Helsing left Mina asleep and made his way to the fearful castle. The doors were open, but he broke off their hinges with a hammer to make sure he would not be trapped inside. Then he began his search.

As he found the first grave, he heard, far off,

He Broke Off Their Hinges.

the howl of a wolf. Should he return to Mina? No, he thought. Better that she should be eaten by wolves. He could not leave this work undone.

Inside the grave, looking very, very beautiful, was the first of the three women. As he gazed on her lovely face, Van Helsing wondered if he would have the nerve to do what he knew had to be done.

He found the second tomb. The woman who lay inside that one was even more beautiful than the first. And the third tomb held the most radiant woman of all of them. Van Helsing's head began to spin as he thought of what he had to do.

Then he saw a fourth tomb, larger than all the others. On it was carved one word: DRACULA. This was the home of the king of the vampires. And it was, for now, empty. He put garlic on it so that the Count could not use it again.

Now he began the awful work of driving stakes through the bodies of the three women.

With every blow of the hammer, he trembled. The women screeched and plunged and twisted under the stakes. But when the work was done, a look of peace came over each face. Van Helsing finished the job by cutting off the heads of the corpses. Instantly, each body turned to dust.

The professor hurried back to where Mina was waiting. She was awake now, unharmed.

"Hurry," she said. "They are getting close. I know it. We must go and meet them."

They walked down the steep hill. The snowstorm grew worse. It was terribly cold and gray. Behind them, they could see the outline of Castle Dracula, which stood menacingly against the sky.

Mina grew weary with walking through the snow. Van Helsing found a little cave near the side of the road. From it they could look all the way down the side of the mountain. At the bottom they saw the black ribbon of the river. Farther up, they were able to make out a wagon struggling up the mountainside. Behind it, two

Mina Looked at the Distant Figures.

pairs of men on horseback were pursuing the wagon.

"Look through the binoculars and tell me what you see," the professor said.

Mina looked at the distant figures. "On the wagon is a box," she said. "The men around it look like gypsies. They are hurrying. I don't think the men on horseback will catch them."

"The gypsies want to reach the castle before dark," Van Helsing said. "I don't blame them. But they will have to pass here, and we will stop them if we can."

The snow fell more heavily and blotted out the whole scene. When it cleared again, the wagon and those pursuing it were closer.

"It's Jonathan," Mina said. "I can see him clearly now. And Arthur with him. Coming the other way are Dr. Seward and Quincey."

"We will have the gypsies surrounded," Van Helsing said. "Get your pistol ready. I hear the wolves closing in, too."

They waited. They gypsies struggled up the hill. As the snow cleared, the sun came out. It was hanging just above the tops of the mountains. In another few minutes it would set. Then Count Dracula would be free to take on any form he wanted. Their chance to destroy him would be lost, maybe forever.

Just as the gypsies were reaching the spot where Van Helsing and Mina waited, Jonathan, galloping on his horse, caught up with them.

"Halt!" he called. They did not speak English, but they knew from his tone what he was saying. At the same time, Quincey Morris and Dr. Seward appeared on the other side.

The leader of the gypsies gave a command. His men, who surrounded the wagon, urged it on even faster.

The pursuers pointed rifles at the fleeing gypsies. At the same time Van Helsing and Mina, their guns in hand, stepped out from inside the cave.

The gypsies prepared for a fight. Their leader pointed, first at the box on the wagon, then at the setting sun. The battle began.

Jonathan Caught Up with Them.

Jonathan from one side and Quincey from the other began to fight their way toward the wagon. There seemed no way they could reach it before the sun went down. But they continued to struggle. They paid no attention to the flashing knives of the gypsies, nor to the howling of the wolves.

Finally, Jonathan reached the wagon. He leaped up onto it. He lifted the heavy box and flung it over the side.

Quincey and the others continued to fight with the gypsies. One of their knives stabbed toward Quincey, striking him. He grabbed his side. Blood spurted through his fingers.

Still he fought on. He made it to one end of the big box and began to pry it open with his Bowie knife. Jonathan used his own knife to force off the other end. Arthur and Dr. Seward stood guard, forcing the gypsies back.

The cover of the big box fell off. Inside lay Dracula. He was deathly pale. His eyes burned with hatred and evil. But as he saw the sun finally dipping below the mountains, his look turned to one of triumph. He would escape now for sure, he thought.

At that moment, Jonathan's razor-sharp knife cut through the Count's throat. Quincey Morris instantly plunged his big Bowie knife into Dracula's chest.

For an instant a look of deep peace passed over the Count's features. Then his body turned completely to dust.

Seeing this, the gypsies ran for their lives.

Quincey Morris sank to the ground. Blood was still flowing from his wound. Mina ran to him. All the men gathered around.

"Don't grieve, little lady," Quincey said to Mina. "I have my reward. For this, it was worth dying. Look! The curse has passed away."

With his last strength he pointed to where the scar had been on Mina's forehead. The last gleam of the setting sun showed that it was now as pure and white as the snow.

Silently and with a smile, Quincey died.

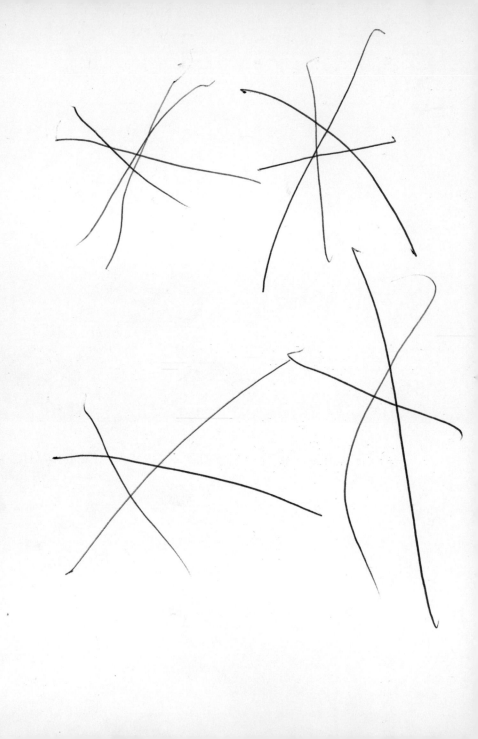